BEST OF
GUY DE MAUPASSANT

One of the greatest French short-story writers, Guy de Maupassant was born on August 5, 1850. He was introduced to the literary circle by his mother's friend, Gustave Flaubert. In 1880, he published his first short story 'Boule de Suif' that received sensational response from readers. His first novel Unne Vie was applauded by Leo Tolstoy as the best French novel since *Les Miserables.*

BEST OF
GUY DE MAUPASSANT

RUPA

Published by
Rupa Publications India Pvt. Ltd 2003
7/16, Ansari Road, Daryaganj
New Delhi 110002

Sales centres:
Allahabad Bengaluru Chennai
Hyderabad Jaipur Kathmandu
Kolkata Mumbai

Edition copyright © Rupa Publications India Pvt. Ltd 2003

This is a work of fiction. Names, characters, places and incidents are either the product of the author's imagination or are used fictitiously, and any resemblance to any actual persons, living or dead, events or locales is entirely coincidental.

All rights reserved.
No part of this publication may be reproduced, transmitted, or stored in a retrieval system, in any form or by any means, electronic, mechanical, photocopying, recording or otherwise, without the prior permission of the publisher.

ISBN: 978-81-291-0129-7

Eighth impression 2022

10 9 8

Printed in India

This book is sold subject to the condition that it shall not, by way of trade or otherwise, be lent, resold, hired out, or otherwise circulated, without the publisher's prior consent, in any form of binding or cover other than that in which it is published.

CONTENTS

Ball-of-Fat	1
A Little Walk	50
The Substitute	58
A Duel	63
The Umbrella	70
An Artifice	81
He?	88
Francis	97
Was it a Dream?	104
The Deaf-Mute	110
Sentiment	121
A Crisis	128
A Normandy Joke	136
Useless Beauty	142
Madame Tellier's Excursion	164

BALL-OF-FAT

FOR MANY DAYS now the fag end of the army had been straggling through the town. They were not troops but a disbanded horde. The beards of the men were long and filthy, their uniforms in tatters, and they advanced at an easy pace without flag or regiment. All seemed worn out and back broken, incapable of a thought or a resolution, marching by habit solely and falling from fatigue as soon as they stopped. In short, they were a mobilized, pacific people, bending under the weight of the gun; some little squads on the alert, easy to take alarm and prompt in enthusiasm, ready to attack or to flee; and in the midst of them some red breeches, the remains of a division broken up in a great battle; some somber artillerymen in line with these varied kinds of foot soldiers, and sometimes the brilliant helmet of a dragoon on foot who followed with difficulty the shortest march of the lines.

Some legions of free shooters, under the heroic names of Avengers of the Defeat, Citizens of the Tomb, Partakers of Death, passed in their turn with the air of bandits.

Their leaders were former cloth or grain merchants, ex-merchants in tallow or soap, warriors of circumstance, elected officers on account of their escutcheons and the length of their mustaches, covered with arms and with braid, speaking in constrained voices, discussing plans of campaign and pretending to carry agonized France alone on their swaggering shoulders but sometimes fearing their own soldiers, prison birds, that were often brave at first and later proved to be plunderers and debauchees.

It was said that the Prussians were going to enter Rouen.

The National Guard who for two months had been carefully reconnoitering in the neighboring woods, shooting sometimes their own sentinels and ready for a combat whenever a little wolf stirred in the thicket, had now returned to their firesides. Their arms, their uniforms, all the murderous accouterments with which they had lately struck fear into the national heart for three leagues in every direction, had suddenly disappeared.

The last French soldiers finally came across the Seine to reach the Audemer bridge through Saint-Sever and Bourg-Achard; and marching behind, on foot, between two officers of ordnance, the general, in despair, unable to do anything with these incongruous tatters, himself lost in the breaking up of a people accustomed to conquer, and disastrously beaten in spite of his legendary bravery.

A profound calm, a frightful, silent expectancy had spread over the city. Many of the heavy citizens, emasculated by commerce, anxiously awaited the conquerors, trembling lest their roasting spits or kitchen knives be considered arms.

All life seemed stopped; shops were closed, the streets dumb. Sometimes an inhabitant, intimidated by this silence, moved rapidly along next the walls. The agony of waiting made them wish the enemy would come.

In the afternoon of the day which followed the departure of the French troops some uhlans, coming from one knows not where, crossed the town with celerity. Then a little later a black mass descended the side of St Catherine, while two other invading bands appeared by the way of Darnetal and Bois-Guillaume. The advance guard of the three bodies joined one another at the same moment in Hôtel de Ville square, and by all the neighboring streets the German army continued to arrive, spreading out its battalions, making the pavement resound under their hard, rhythmic step.

Some orders of the commander, in a foreign, guttural voice, reached the houses which seemed dead and deserted, while behind closed shutters eyes were watching these victorious men, masters of the city, of fortunes, of lives, through the "rights of war." The inhabitants, shut up in their rooms, were visited with the kind of excitement that a cataclysm or some fatal upheaval of the earth brings to us, against which all force is useless. For the same sensation is produced each time that the established order of things is over-turned, when security no longer exists and all that protect the laws of man and of nature find themselves at the mercy of unreasoning, ferocious brutality. The trembling of the earth crushing the houses and burying an entire people; a river overflowing its banks and carrying in its course the drowned peasants, carcasses of beeves and girders snatched from roofs, or a glorious army massacring those trying to defend themselves, leading other prisoners, pillaging in the name of the sword and thanking God to the sound of the cannon; all are alike frightful scourges which disconnect all belief in eternal justice, all the confidence that we have in the protection of Heaven and the reason of man.

Some detachments rapped at each door, then disappeared into the houses. It was occupation after invasion. Then the duty commences for the conquered to show themselves gracious toward the conquerors.

After some time, as soon as the first terror disappears, a new calm is established. In many families the Prussian officer eats at the table. He is sometimes well bred and, through politeness, pities France and speaks of his repugnance in taking part in this affair. One is grateful to him for this sentiment; then, one may be, someday or other, in need of his protection. By treating him well one has, perhaps, a less number of men to feed. And why should we wound anyone on whom we are entirely dependent? To act thus would be less bravery than temerity. And temerity is no longer a fault of the commoner of Rouen as it was at the time of the heroic defense when their city became famous. Finally each told himself that the highest judgment of French urbanity required that they be allowed to be polite to the strange soldier in the house, provided they did not show themselves familiar with him in public. Outside they would not make themselves known to each other, but at home they could chat freely, and the German might remain longer each evening warming his feet at their hearthstones.

The town even took on, little by little, its ordinary aspect. The French scarcely went out, but the Prussian soldiers grumbled in the streets. In short, the officers of the Blue Hussars, who dragged with arrogance their great weapons of death up and down the pavement, seemed to have no more grievous scorn for the simple citizens than the officers or the sportsmen who, the year before, drank in the same cafés.

There was, nevertheless, something in the air, something subtle and unknown, a strange, intolerable atmosphere like a penetrating odor, the odor of invasion. It filled the dwellings and the public places, changed the taste of the food, gave the impression of being on a journey, far away among barbarous and dangerous tribes.

The conquerors exacted money, much money. The

inhabitants always paid and they were rich enough to do it. But the richer a trading Norman becomes the more he suffers at every outlay, at each part of his fortune that he sees pass from his hands into those of another.

Therefore, two or three leagues below the town, following the course of the river toward Croisset, Dieppedalle or Biessard, mariners and fishermen often picked up the swollen corpse of a German in uniform from the bottom of the river, killed by the blow of a knife, the head crushed with a stone, or perhaps thrown into the water by a push from the high bridge. The slime of the river bed buried these obscure vengeances, savage but legitimate, unknown heroisms, mute attacks more perilous than the battles of broad day and without the echoing sound of glory.

For hatred of the foreigner always arouses some intrepid ones who are ready to die for an idea.

Finally, as soon as the invaders had brought the town quite under subjection with their inflexible discipline, without having been guilty of any of the horrors for which they were famous along their triumphal line of march people began to take courage, and the need of trade put new heart into the commerce of the country. Some had large interests at Havre, which the French army occupied, and they wished to try and reach this port by going to Dieppe by land and there embarking.

They used their influence with the German soldiers with whom they had an acquaintance, and finally an authorization of departure was obtained from the general in chief.

Then, a large diligence with four horses having been engaged for this journey, and ten persons having engaged seats in it, it was resolved to set out on Tuesday morning before daylight, in order to escape observation.

For some time before, the frost had been hardening the earth, and on Monday, toward three o'clock, great black clouds coming from the north brought the snow which fell without interruption during the evening and all night.

At half-past four in the morning the travelers met in the courtyard of Hôtel Normandie, where they were to take the carriage.

They were still full of sleep and shivering with cold under their wraps. They could only see each other dimly in the obscure light, and the accumulation of heavy winter garments made them all resemble fat curates in long cassocks. Only two of the men were acquainted; a third accosted them and they chatted: "I'm going to take my wife," said one. "I too," said another. "And I," said the third. The first added: "We shall not return to Rouen, and if the Prussians approach Havre, we shall go over to England." All had the same projects, being of the same mind.

As yet the horses were not harnessed. A little lantern, carried by a stable-boy, went out one door from time to time, to immediately appear at another. The feet of the horses striking the floor could be heard, although deadened by the straw and litter, and the voice of a man talking to the beasts, sometimes swearing, came from the end of the building. A light tinkling of bells announced that they were taking down the harness; this murmur soon became a clear and continuous rhythm by the movement of the animal, stopping sometimes, then breaking into a brusque shake which was accompanied by the dull stamp of a sabot upon the hard earth.

The door suddenly closed. All noise ceased. The frozen

citizens were silent; they remained immovable and stiff.

A curtain of uninterrupted white flakes constantly sparkled in its descent to the ground. It effaced forms and powdered everything with a downy moss. And nothing could be heard in the great silence. The town was calm and buried under the wintry frost as this fall of snow, unnamable and floating, a sensation rather than a sound (trembling atoms which only seem to fill all space), came to cover the earth.

The man reappeared with his lantern, pulling at the end of a rope a sad horse which would not come willingly. He placed him against the pole, fastened the traces, walked about a long time adjusting the harness, for he had the use of but one hand, the other carrying the lantern. As he went for the second horse he noticed the travelers, motionless, already white with snow, and said to them: "Why not get into the carriage? You will be under cover at least."

They had evidently not thought of it, and they hastened to do so. The three men installed their wives at the back and then followed them. Then the other forms, undecided and veiled, took in their turn the last places without exchanging a word.

The floor was covered with straw, in which the feet ensconced themselves. The ladies at the back having brought little copper foot stoves, with a carbon fire, lighted them and for some time, in low voices, enumerated the advantages of the appliances, repeating things that they had known for a long time.

Finally the carriage was harnessed with six horses instead of four, because the traveling was very bad, and a voice called out:

"Is everybody aboard?"

And a voice within answered: "Yes."

They were off. The carriage moved slowly, slowly for a little way. The wheels were imbedded in the snow; the whole body groaned with heavy cracking sounds; the horses glistened, puffed and smoked; and the great whip of the driver snapped without ceasing, hovering about on all sides, knotting and unrolling itself like a thin serpent, lashing brusquely some horse on the rebound, which then put forth its most violent effort.

Now the day was imperceptibly dawning. The light flakes, which one of the travelers, a Rouenese by birth, said looked like a shower of cotton, no longer fell. A faint light filtered through the great dull clouds, which rendered more brilliant the white of the fields, where appeared a line of great trees clothed in whiteness or a chimney with a cap of snow.

In the carriage each looked at the others curiously in the sad light of this dawn.

At the back, in the best places, M. Loiseau, wholesale merchant of wine, of Grand-Pont Street, and Mme Loiseau were sleeping opposite each other. Loiseau had bought out his former patron, who failed in business, and made his fortune. He sold bad wine at a good price to small retailers in the country and passed among his friends and acquaintances as a knavish wag, a true Norman full of deceit and joviality.

His reputation as a sharper was so well established that one evening at the residence of the prefect, M. Tournel, author of some fables and songs, of keen, satirical mind, a local celebrity, having proposed to some ladies, who seemed to be getting a little sleepy, that they make up a game of "Loiseau tricks," the joke traversed the rooms of the prefect, reached those of the town and then, in the months to come, made many a face in the province expand with laughter.

Loiseau was especially known for his love of farce of every kind, for his jokes, good and bad; and no one could ever talk with him without thinking. "He is invaluable, this Loiseau." Of tall figure, his balloon-shaped front was surmounted by a ruddy face surrounded by gray whiskers.

His wife, large, strong and resolute, with a quick, decisive manner, was the order and arithmetic of this house of commerce, while he was the life of it through his joyous activity.

Beside them M. Carré-Lamadon held himself with great dignity, as if belonging to a superior caste; a considerable man in cottons, proprietor of three mills, officer of the Legion of Honor and member of the General Council. He had remained, during the Empire, chief of the friendly opposition, famous for making the emperor pay more dear for rallying to the cause than if he had combated it with blunted arms, according to his own story. Mme Carré-Lamadon, much younger than her husband, was the consolation of officers of good family sent to Rouen in garrison. She sat opposite her husband, very dainty, petite and pretty, wrapped closely in furs and looking with sad eyes at the interior of the carriage.

Her neighbors, the Count and Countess Hubert de Breville, bore the name of one of the most ancient and noble families of Normandy. The count, an old gentleman of good figure, accentuated by the artifices of his toilette his resemblance to King Henry IV. who, following a glorious legend of the family, had impregnated one of the De Breville ladies, whose husband, for this reason was made a count and governor of the province.

A colleague of M. Carré-Lamadon in the General

Council, Count Hubert represented the Orléans party in the department.

The story of his marriage with the daughter of a little captain of a privateer had always remained a mystery. But as the countess had a grand air, received better than anyone and passed for having been loved by the son of Louis Philippe, all the nobility did her honor, and her salon remained the first in the country, the only one which preserved the old gallantry and to which the entree was difficult. The fortune of the Brevilles amounted, it was said, to five hundred thousand francs in income, all in good securities.

These six persons formed the foundation of the carriage company, the society side, serene and strong, honest, established people, who had both religion and principles.

By a strange chance all the women were upon the same seat, and the countess had for neighbors two sisters who picked at long strings of beads and muttered some "Paters" and "Aves." One was old and as pitted with small-pox as if she had received a broadside of grapeshot full in the face. The other, very sad, had a pretty face and a disease of the lungs, which, added to their devoted faith, illumined them and made them appear like martyrs.

Opposite these two devotees were a man and a woman who attracted the notice of all. The man, well known, was Cornudet the democrat, the terror of respectable people. For twenty years he had soaked his great red beard in the bocks of all the democratic cafés. He had consumed with his friends and confreres a rather pretty fortune left him by his father, an old confectioner, and he awaited the establishing of the Republic with impatience, that he might have the position he merited by his great expenditures. On the fourth of September, by some joke perhaps, he believed himself elected prefect, but when he went to assume the duties the clerks of the office were masters of the place and refused to recognize him, obliging him to retreat. Rather a good bachelor on the whole, inoffensive and serviceable, he had busied himself, with incomparable ardor, in organizing the defense against the Prussians. He had dug holes in all the plains, cut down young trees from the neighboring forests, sown snares over all routes and, at the approach of the enemy, took himself quickly back to the town. He now thought he could be of more use in Havre, where more entrenchments would be necessary.

The woman, one of those called a coquette, was celebrated for the *embonpoint*, which had given her the nick-name of "Ball-of-Fat." Small, round and fat as lard, with puffy fingers choked at the phalanges like chaplets of short sausages, with a stretched and shining skin, an enormous bosom which shook under her dress, she was, nevertheless, pleasing and sought after on account of a certain freshness and breeziness of disposition. Her face was a round apple, a peony bud ready to pop into bloom, and inside that opened two great black eyes shaded with thick brows that cast a shadow within; and below, a charming mouth, humid for kissing, furnished with shining microscopic baby teeth. She was, it was said, full of admirable qualities.

As soon as she was recognized a whisper went around among the honest women, and the words "prostitute" and "public shame" were whispered so loud that she raised her head. Then she threw at her neighbors such a provoking, courageous look that a great silence reigned, and everybody looked down except Loiseau, who watched her with an exhilarated air.

And immediately conversation began among the three

ladies, whom the presence of this girl had suddenly rendered friendly, almost intimate. It seemed to them they should bring their married dignity into union in opposition to that sold without shame; for legal love always takes on a tone of contempt for its free confrere.

The three men, also drawn together by an instinct of preservation at the sight of Cornudet, talked money with a certain high tone of disdain for the poor. Count Hubert talked of the havoc which the Prussians had caused, the losses which resulted from being robbed of cattle and from destroyed crops, with the assurance of a great lord, ten times millionaire, whom these ravages would scarcely cramp for a year. M. Carré-Lamadon, largely experienced in the cotton industry, had had need of sending six hundred thousand francs to England, as a trifle in reserve if it should be needed. As for Loiseau, he had arranged with the French administration to sell them all the wines that remained in his cellars, on account of which the State owned him a formidable sum which he counted on collecting at Havre.

And all three threw toward each other swift and amicable glances.

Although in different conditions, they felt themselves to be brothers through money, that grand freemasonry of those who possess it and make the gold rattle by putting their hands in their trousers' pockets.

The carriage went so slowly that at ten o'clock in the morning they had not gone four leagues. The men had got down three times to climb hills on foot. They began to be disturbed because they should be now taking breakfast at Tôtes, and they despaired now of reaching there before night. Each one had begun to watch for an inn along the route, when the carriage foundered in a snowdrift and it took two hours to extricate it.

Growing appetites troubled their minds; and no eating house, no wineshop showed itself, the approach of the passage of the troops having frightened away all these industries.

The gentlemen ran to the farms along the way for provisions, but they did not even find bread, for the defiant peasant had concealed his stores for fear of being pillaged by the soldiers who, having nothing to put between their teeth, took by force whatever they discovered.

Toward one o'clock in the afternoon Loiseau announced that there was a decided hollow in his stomach. Everybody suffered with him, and the violent need of eating, ever increasing, had killed conversation.

From time to time someone yawned; another immediately imitated him; and each, in his turn, in accordance with his character, his knowledge of life and his social position, opened his mouth with carelessness or modesty, placing his hand quickly before the yawning hole from whence issued a vapor.

Ball-of-Fat, after many attempts, bent down as if seeking something under her skirts. She hesitated a second, looked at her neighbors, then sat up again tranquilly. The faces were pale and drawn. Loiseau affirmed that he would give a thousand francs for a small ham. His wife made a gesture as if in protest, but she kept quiet. She was always troubled when anyone spoke of squandering money and could not comprehend any pleasantry on the subject. "The fact is," said the count, "I cannot understand why I did not think to bring some provisions with me." Each reproached himself in the same way.

However, Cornudet had a flask full of rum. He offered it; it was refused coldly. Loiseau alone accepted two swallows and then passed back the flask saying, by way of thanks: "It is good all the same; it is warming and checks the appetite." The alcohol put him in good humor, and he proposed that they do as they did on the little ship in the song, eat the fattest of the passengers. This indirect allusion to Ball-of-Fat choked the well-bred people. They said nothing. Cornudet alone laughed. The two good sisters had ceased to mumble their rosaries and, with their hands enfolded in their great sleeves, held themselves immovable, obstinately lowering their eyes, without doubt offering to Heaven the suffering it had brought upon them.

Finally at three o'clock, when they found themselves in the midst of an interminable plain, without a single village in sight, Ball-of-Fat, bending down quickly, drew from under the seat a large basket covered with a white napkin.

At first she brought out a little china plate and a silver cup, then a large dish in which there were two whole chickens, cut up and imbedded in their own jelly. And one could still see in the basket other good things, some *pâtés*, fruits and sweetmeats, provisions for three days if they should not see the kitchen of an inn. Four necks of bottles were seen among the packages of food. She took a wing of a chicken and began to eat it delicately with one of those biscuits called "Regence" in Normandy.

All looks were turned in her direction. Then the odor spread, enlarging the nostrils and making the mouth water, besides causing a painful contraction of the jaw behind the ears. The scorn of the women for this girl became ferocious, as if they had a desire to kill her and throw her out of the carriage into the snow, her silver cup, her basket, provisions and all.

But Loiseau with his eyes devoured the dish of chicken.

He said: "Fortunately Madame had more precaution than we. There are some people who know how to think ahead always."

She turned toward him, saying: "If you would like some of it, sir? It is hard to go without breakfast so long."

He saluted her and replied: "Faith, I frankly cannot refuse; I can stand it no longer. Everything goes in time of war, does it not, Madame?" And then, casting a comprehensive glance around, he added: "In moments like this, one can but be pleased to find people who are obliging."

He had a newspaper which he spread out on his knees that no spot might come to his pantaloons, and upon the point of a knife that he always carried in his pocket he took up a leg all glistening with jelly, put it between his teeth and masticated it with a satisfaction so evident that there ran through the carriage a great sigh of distress.

Then Ball-of-Fat, in a sweet and humble voice, proposed that the two sisters partake of her collation. They both accepted instantly and, without raising their eyes, began to eat very quickly, after stammering their thanks. Cornudet no longer refused the offers of his neighbor, and they formed with the sisters a sort of table, by spreading out some newspapers upon their knees.

The mouths opened and shut without ceasing; they masticated, swallowed, gulping ferociously. Loiseau in his corner was working hard and, in a low voice, was trying to induce his wife to follow his example. She resisted for a long time; then, when a drawn sensation ran through her body, she yielded. Her husband, rounding his phrase, asked their "charming companion" if he might he allowed to offer a little piece to Mme Loiseau.

She replied: "Why, yes, certainly, sir," with an amiable

smile as she passed the dish.

An embarrassing thing confronted them when they opened the first bottle of Bordeaux: they had but one cup. Each passed it after having tasted. Cornudet alone, for politeness without about, placed his lips at the spot left humid by his fair neighbor.

Then, surrounded by people eating, suffocated by the odors of the food, the Count and Countess de Breville, as well as Mme and M. Carré-Lamadon, were suffering that odious torment which has preserved the name of Tantalus. Suddenly the young wife of the manufacturer gave forth such a sigh that all heads were turned in her direction; she was as white as the snow without; her eyes closed, her head drooped; she had lost consciousness. Her husband, much excited, implored the help of everybody. Each lost his head completely, until the elder of the two sisters, holding the head of the sufferer, slipped Ball-of-Fat's cup between her lips and forced her to swallow a few drops of wine. The pretty little lady revived, opened her eyes, smiled and declared in a dying voice that she felt very well now. But, in order that the attack might not return, the sister urged her to drink a full glass of Bordeaux and added: "It is just hunger, nothing more."

Then Ball-of-Fat, blushing and embarrassed, looked at the four travelers who had fasted and stammered: "Goodness knows! if I dared to offer anything to these gentlemen and ladies, I would —" Then she was silent, as if fearing an insult. Loiseau took up the word: "Ah! certainly in times like these all the world are brothers and ought to aid each other. Come, ladies, without ceremony; why the devil not accept? We do not know whether we shall even find a house where we can pass the night. At the pace we are going now we shall not reach Tôtes before noon tomorrow."

They still hesitated, no one daring to assume the responsibility of a "Yes." The count decided the question. He turned toward the fat, intimidated girl and, taking on a grand air of condescension, he said to her:

"We accept with gratitude, madame."

It is the first step that counts. The Rubicon passed, one lends himself to the occasion squarely. The basket was stripped. It still contained a *pâté de foie gras*, a *pâté* of larks, a piece of smoked tongue, some preserved pears, a loaf of hard bread, some wafers and a full cup of pickled gherkins and onions, of which crudities Ball-of-Fat, like all women, was extremely fond.

They could not eat this girl's provisions without speaking to her. And so they chatted, with reserve at first; then, as she carried herself well, with more abandon. The ladies De Breville and Carré-Lamadon, who were acquainted with all the ins and outs of good breeding, were gracious with a certain delicacy. The countess, especially, showed that amiable condescension of very noble ladies who do not fear being spoiled by contact with anyone and was charming. But the great Mme Loiseau, who had the soul of a plebeian, remained crabbed, saying little and eating much.

The conversation was about the war, naturally. They related the horrible deeds of the Prussians, the brave acts of the French; and all of them, although running away, did homage to those who stayed behind. Then personal stories began to be told, and Ball-of-Fat related, with sincere emotion and in the heated words that such girls sometimes use in expressing their natural feelings, how she had left Rouen:

"I believed at first that I could remain," she said. "I

had my house full of provisions, and I preferred to feed a few soldiers rather than expatriate myself, to go I knew not where. But as soon as I saw them, those Prussians, that was too much for me! They made my blood boil with anger, and I wept for very shame all day long. Oh! if I were only a man! I watched them from my windows, the great porkers with their pointed helmets, and my maid held my hands to keep me from throwing the furniture down upon them. Then one of them came to lodge at my house; I sprang at his throat the first thing; they are no more difficult to strangle than other people. And I should have put an end to that one then and there had they not pulled me away by the hair. After that it was necessary to keep out of sight. And finally, when I found an opportunity, I left town and—here I am!"

They congratulated her. She grew in the estimation of her companions, who had not shown themselves so hot-brained, and Cornudet, while listening to her, took on the approving, benevolent smile of an apostle, as a priest would if he heard a devotee praise God, for the long-bearded democrats have a monopoly of patriotism, as the men in cassocks have of religion. In his turn he spoke in a doctrinal tone, with the emphasis of a proclamation such as we see pasted on the walls about town, and finished by a bit of eloquence whereby he gave that "scamp of a Badinguet" a good lashing.

Then Ball-of-Fat was angry, for she was a Bonapartist. She grew redder than a cherry and, stammering with indignation, said:

"I would like to have seen you in his place, you other people. Then everything would have been quite right; oh yes! It is you who have betrayed this man! One would never have had to leave France if it had been governed by blackguards like you!"

Cornudet, undisturbed, preserved a disdainful, superior smile, but all felt that the high note had been struck, until the count, not without some difficulty, calmed the exasperated girl and proclaimed with a manner of authority that all sincere opinions should be respected. But the countess and the manufacturer's wife, who had in their souls an unreasonable hatred for the people that favor a republic and the same instinctive tenderness that all women have for a decorative, despotic government, felt themselves drawn, in spite of themselves, toward this prostitute so full of dignity, whose sentiments so strongly resembled their own.

The basket was empty. By ten o'clock they had easily exhausted the contents and regretted that there was not more. Conversation continued for some time, but a little more coldly since they had finished eating.

The night fell; the darkness little by little became profound, and the cold, felt more during digestion, made Ball-of-Fat shiver in spite of her plumpness. Then Mme de Breville offered her the little foot stove, in which the fuel had been renewed many times since morning; she accepted it immediately, for her feet were becoming numb with cold. The ladies Carré-Lamadon and Loiseau gave theirs to the two religious sisters.

The driver had lighted his lanterns. They shone out with a lively glimmer, showing a cloud of foam beyond, the sweat of the horses; and, on both sides of the way, the snow seemed to roll itself along under the moving reflection of the lights.

Inside the carriage one could distinguish nothing. But a sudden movement seemed to be made between Ball-of-Fat and Cornuder; and Loiseau, whose eye penetrated the shadow, believed that he saw the big-bearded man start back quickly as if he had received a swift, noiseless blow.

Then some twinkling points of fire appeared in the distance along the road. It was Tôtes. They had traveled eleven hours, which, with the two hours given to resting and feeding the horses, made thirteen. They entered the town and stopped before the Hotel of Commerce.

The carriage door opened! A well-known sound gave the travelers a start; it was the scabbard of a sword hitting the ground. Immediately a German voice was heard in the darkness.

Although the diligence was not moving, no one offered to alight, fearing someone might be waiting to murder them as they stepped out. Then the conductor appeared, holding in his hand one of the lanterns which lighted the carriage to its depth and showed the two rows of frightened faces whose mouths were open and whose eyes were wide with surprise and fear.

Outside, beside the driver, in plain sight stood a German officer, an excessively tall young man, thin and blond, squeezed into his uniform like a girl in a corset and wearing on his head a flat oilcloth cap which made him resemble the porter of an English hotel. His enormous mustache, of long straight hairs, growing gradually thin at each side and terminating in a single blond thread so fine that one could not perceive where it ended, seemed to weight heavily on the corners of his mouth and, drawing down the cheeks, left a decided wrinkle about the lips.

In Alsatian French he invited the travelers to come in, saying in a suave tone: "Will you descend, gentlemen and ladies?"

The two good sisters were the first to obey, with the docility of saints accustomed ever to submission. The count and countess then appeared, followed by the manufacturer and his wife; then Loiseau, pushing ahead of him his larger half. The last named, as he set foot on the earth, said to the officer: "Good evening, sir," more as a measure of prudence than politeness. The officer, insolent as all powerful people usually are, looked at him without a word.

Ball-of-Fat and Cornudet, although nearest the door, were the last to descend, grave and haughty before the enemy. The fat girl tried to control herself and be calm. The democrat waved a tragic hand, and his long beard seemed to tremble a little and grow redder. They wished to preserve their dignity, comprehending that in such meetings as these they represented in some degree their great country; and somewhat disgusted with the docility of her companions, the fat girl tried to show more pride than her neighbors, the honest women, and as she felt that someone should set an example she continued her attitude of resistance assumed at the beginning of the journey.

They entered the vast kitchen of the inn, and the German, having demanded their traveling papers signed by the General in chief (in which the name, the description and profession of each traveler was mentioned) and having examined them all critically, comparing the people and their signatures, said: "It is quite right," and went out.

Then they breathed. They were still hungry and supper was ordered. A half-hour was necessary to prepare it, and while two servants were attending to this they went to their rooms. They found them along a corridor which terminated in a large glazed door.

Finally they sat down at table, when the proprietor of the inn himself appeared. He was a former horse merchant, a large, asthmatic man with a constant wheezing and rattling in his throat. His father had left him the name of Follenvie. He asked:

"Is Miss Elizabeth Rousset here?"

Ball-of-Fat started as she answered: "It is I."

"The Prussian officer wishes to speak with you immediately."

"With me?"

"Yes, that is, if you are Miss Elizabeth Rousset."

She was disturbed and, reflecting for an instant, declared flatly:

"That is my name, but I shall not go."

A stir was felt around her; each discussed and tried to think of the cause of this order. The count approached her, saying:

"You are wrong, Madame, for your refusal may lead to considerable difficulty, not only for yourself but for all your companions. It is never worth while to resist those in power. This request cannot assuredly bring any danger; it is, without doubt, about some forgotten formality."

Everybody agreed with him, asking, begging, beseeching her to go, and at last they convinced her that it was best; they all feared the complications that might result from disobedience. She finally said:

"It is for you that I do this, you understand."

The countess took her by the hand, saying: "And we are grateful to you for it."

She went out. They waited before sitting down at table.

Each one regretted not having been sent for in the place of this violent, irascible girl and mentally prepared some platitudes in case they should be called in their turn.

But at the end of ten minutes she reappeared, out of breath, red to suffocation and exasperated. She stammered: "Oh! the rascal; the rascal!"

All gathered around to learn something, but she said

nothing; and when the count insisted she responded with great dignity: "No, it does not concern you; I can say nothing."

Then they all seated themselves around a high soup tureen whence came the odor of cabbage. In spite of alarm the supper was gay. The cider was good; the beverage Loiseau and the good sisters took as a means of economy. The others called for wine; Cornudet demanded beer. He had a special fashion of uncorking the bottle, making froth on the liquid, carefully filling the glass and then holding it before the light to better appreciate the color. When he drank, his great beard, which still kept some of the foam of his beloved beverage, seemed to tremble with tenderness; his eyes were squinted, in order not to lose sight of his tipple, and he had the unique air of fulfilling the function for which he was born. One would say that there was in his mind a meeting, like that of affinities, between the two great passions that occupied his life—Pale Ale and Revolutions; and assuredly he could not taste the one without thinking of the other.

M. and Mme Follenvie dined at the end of the table. The man, rattling like a cracked locomotive, had too much trouble in breathing to talk while eating, but his wife was never silent. She told all her impressions at the arrival of the Prussians, what they did, what they said, reviling them because they cost her some money and because she had two sons in the army. She addressed herself especially to the countess, flattered by being able to talk with a lady of quality.

When she lowered her voice to say some delicate thing her husband would interrupt, from time to time, with: "You had better keep silent, Madame Follenvie." But she paid no attention, continuing in this fashion:

"Yes, madame, those people there not only eat our potatoes and pork but our pork and potatoes. And it must not be believed that they are at all proper —oh no! Such filthy things they do, saving the respect I owe to you! And if you could see them exercise for hours in the day! They are all there in the field, marching ahead, then marching back, turning here and turning there. They might be cultivating the land or at least working on the roads of their own country! But no, madame, these military men are profitable to no one. Poor people have to feed them or perhaps be murdered! I am only an old woman without education, it is true, but when I see some endangering their constitutions by raging from morning to night I say. 'When there are so many people found to be useless, how unnecessary it is for others to take so much trouble to be nuisances!' Truly, is it not an abomination to kill people, whether they be Prussian or English or Polish or French? If one man revenges himself upon another who has done him some injury, it is wicked and he is punished; but when they exterminate our boys as if they were game, with guns, they give decorations, indeed, to the one who destroys the most! Now, you see, I can never understand that, never!"

Cornudet raised his voice: "War is a barbarity when one attacks a peaceable neighbor but a sacred duty when one defends his country."

The old woman lowered her head.

"Yes, when one defends himself it is another thing; but why not make it a duty to kill all the kings who make these wars for their pleasure?"

Cornudet's eyes flashed. "Bravo, my countrywoman!" said he.

M. Carré-Lamadon reflected profoundly. Although he

was prejudiced as a captain of industry, the good sense of this peasant woman made him think of the opulence that would be brought into the country were the idle and consequently mischievous hands, and the troops which were now maintained in unproductiveness, employed in some great industrial work that it would require centuries to achieve.

Loiseau, leaving his place, went to speak with the innkeeper in a low tone of voice. The great man laughed, shook and squeaked, his corpulence quivered with joy at the jokes of his neighbor, and he bought of him six cases of wine for spring, after the Prussians had gone.

As soon as supper was finished, as they were worn out with fatigue, they retired.

However, Loiseau, who had observed things, after getting his wife to bed glued his eyes and then his ear to a hole in the wall to try and discover what are known as "the mysteries of the corridor."

At the end of about an hour he heard a groping and, looking quickly, he perceived Ball-of-Fat, who appeared still more plump in a blue cashmere negligee trimmed with white lace. She had a candle in her hand and was directing her steps toward the great door at the end of the corridor. But a door at the side opened, and when she returned at the end of some minutes Cornudet, in his suspenders, followed her. They spoke low, then they stopped. Ball-of-Fat seemed to be defending the entrance to her room with energy. Loiseau, unfortunately, could not hear all their words, but finally, as they raised their voices, he was able to catch a few. Cornudet insisted with vivacity. He said:

"Come, now, you are silly woman; what harm can be done?"

She had an indignant air in responding: "No, my dear, there are moments when such things are out of place. Here it would be a shame."

He doubtless did not comprehend and asked why. Then she cried out, raising her voice still more:

"Why? You do not see why? When there are Prussians in the house, in the very next room, perhaps?"

He was silent. This patriotic shame of the harlot, who would not suffer his caress so near the enemy, must have awakened the latent dignity in his heart, for after simply kissing her he went back to his own door with a bound. Loiseau, much excited, left the aperture, cut a caper in his room, put on his pajamas, turned back the clothes that covered the bony carcass of his companion, whom he awakened with a kiss, murmuring: "Do you love me, dearie?"

Then all the house was still. And immediately there arose somewhere, from an uncertain quarter which might be the cellar but was quite as likely to be the garret, a powerful snoring, monotonous and regular, a heavy, prolonged sound, like a great kettle under pressure. M. Follenvie was asleep.

As they had decided that they would set out at eight o'clock the next morning, they all collected in the kitchen. But the carriage, the roof of which was covered with snow, stood undisturbed in the courtyard, without horses and without a conductor. They sought him in vain in the stables, in the hay and in the coach house. Then they resolved to scour the town and started out. They found themselves in a square, with a church at one end and some low houses on either side, where they perceived some Prussian soldiers. The first one they saw was paring potatoes. The second, further off, was cleaning the hairdresser's shop. Another, bearded to the eyes, was tending a troublesome brat, cradling it and trying to appease it; and the great peasant women, whose husbands were "away in the army," indicated by signs to their obedient conquerors the work they wished to have done: cutting wood, cooking the soup, grinding the coffee or what not. One of them even washed the linen of his hostess, an impotent old grandmother.

The count, astonished, asked questions of the beadle who came out of the rectory. The old man responded:

"Oh! those men are not wicked; they are not the Prussians we hear about. They are from far off, I know not where; and they have left wives and children in their country; it is not amusing to them, this war, I can tell you! I am sure they also weep for their homes and that it makes as much sorrow among them as it does among us. Here, now, there is not so much unhappiness for the moment, because the soldiers do no harm and they work as if they were in their own homes. You see, sir, among poor people it is necessary that they aid one another. These are the great traits which war develops."

Cornudet, indignant at the cordial relations between the conquerors and the conquered, preferred to shut himself up in the inn. Loiseau had a joke for the occasion: "The will repeople the land."

M. Carré-Lamadon had a serious word: "They try to make amends."

But they did not find the driver. Finally they discovered him in a café of the village, sitting at table fraternally with the officer of ordnance. The count called out to him:

"Were you not ordered to be ready at eight o'clock?"

"Well, yes; but another order has been given me since."

"By whom?"

"Faith! the Prussian commander."

"What was it?"

"Not to harness at all."

"Why?"

"I know nothing about it. Go and ask him. They tell me not to harness, and I don't harness. That's all."

"Did he give you the order himself?"

"No sir, the innkeeper gave the order for him."

"When was that?"

"Last evening, as I was going to bed."

The three men returned, much disturbed. They asked for M. Follenvie, but the servant answered that that gentleman, because of his asthma, never rose before ten o'clock. And he had given strict orders not to be wakened before that, except in case of fire.

They wished to see the officer, but that was absolutely impossible since, while he lodged at the inn, M. Follenvie alone was authorized to speak to him upon civil affairs. So they waited. The women went up to their rooms again and occupied themselves with futile tasks.

Cornudet installed himself near the great chimney in the kitchen, where there was a good fire burning. He ordered one of the little tables to be brought from the café, then a can of beer; he then drew out his pipe, which plays among democrats a part almost equal to his own, because in serving Cornudert it was serving its country. It was a superb pipe, an admirably colored meer-schaum, as black as the teeth of its master, but perfumed, curved, glistening, easy to the hand, completing his physiognomy. And he remained motionless, his eyes as much fixed upon the flame of the fire as upon his favorite tipple and its frothy crown; and each time that he drank he passed his long thin fingers through his scanty gray hair with an air of satisfaction, after which he sucked in his mustache fringed with foam.

Loiseau, under the pretext of stretching his legs, were to place some wine among the retailers of the country. The count and the manufacturer began to talk politics. They could foresee the future of France. One of them believed in an Orléans, the other in some unknown savior for the country, a hero who would reveal himself when all were in despair: a Guesclin or a Joan of Arc, perhaps, or would it be another Napoleon First? Ah! if the Prince Imperial were not so young!

Cornudet listened to them and smiled like one who holds the word of destiny. His pipe perfumed the kitchen.

As ten o'clock struck M. Follenvie appeared. They asked him hurried questions, but he could only repeat two or three times, without variation, these words:

"The officer said to me: Monsieur Follenvie, you see to it that the carriage is not harnessed for those travelers tomorrow. I do not wish them to leave without my order. That is sufficient."

Then they wished to see the officer. The count sent him his card, on which M. Carré-Lamadon wrote his name and all his titles. The Prussian sent back word that he would meet the two gentlemen after he had breakfasted, that is to say, about one o'clock.

The ladies reappeared and ate a little something, despite their disquiet. Ball-of-Fat seemed ill and prodigiously troubled.

They were finishing their coffee when the word came that the officer was ready to meet the gentlemen. Loiseau joined them; but when they tried to enlist Cornudet, to give more solemnity to their proceedings, he declared proudly that he would have nothing to do with the

Germans, and he betook himself to his chimney corner and ordered another liter of beer.

The three men mounted the staircase and were introduced to the best room of the inn, where the officer received them, stretched out in an armchair, his feet on the mantelpiece, smoking a long porcelain pipe and enveloped in a flamboyant dressing gown, appropriated, without doubt, from some dwelling belonging to a common citizen of bad taste. He did not rise nor greet them in any way, not even looking at them. It was a magnificent display of natural blackguardism transformed into the military victor.

At the expiration of some moments he asked: "What is it you wish?"

The count became spokesman: "We desire to go on our way, sir."

"No."

"May I ask the cause of this refusal?"

"Because I do not wish it."

"But I would respectfully observe to you, sir, that your general in chief gave us permission to go to Dieppe, and I know of nothing we have done to merit your severity."

"I do not wish it—that is all; you can go."

All three, having bowed, retired.

The afternoon was lamentable. They could not understand this caprice of the German, and the most singular ideas would come into their heads to trouble them. Everybody stayed in the kitchen and discussed the situation endlessly, imagining all sorts of unlikely things. Perhaps they would be retained as hostages—but to what end?—or taken prisoners—or rather a considerable ransom might be demanded. At this thought a panic prevailed. The richest were the most frightened, already seeing themselves constrained to pay for their lives with sacks of gold poured into the hands of this insolent soldier. They racked their brains to think of some acceptable falsehoods to conceal their riches and make them pass themselves off for poor people, very poor people. Loiseau took off the chain to his watch and hid it away in his pocket. The falling night increased their apprehensions. The lamp was lighted, and as there was still two hours before dinner, Mme Loiseau proposed a game of thirty-one. It would be a diversion. They accepted. Cornudet himself having smoked out his pipe, took part for politeness.

The count shuffled the cards, dealt, and Ball-of-Fat had thirty-one at the outset; and immediately the interest was great enough to appease the fear that haunted their minds. Then Cornudet perceived that the house of Loiseau was given to tricks.

As they were going to the dinner table, M. Follenvie again appeared and in wheezing, rattling voice announced:

"The Prussian officer orders me to ask Miss Elizabeth Rousset if she has yet changed her mind."

Ball-of-Fat remained standing and was pale; then, suddenly becoming crimson, such a stifling anger took possession of her that she could not speak. But finally she flashed out: "You may say to the dirty beast, that idiot, that carrion of a Prussian, that I shall never change it; you understand, never, never, never!"

The great innkeeper went out. Then Ball-of-Fat was immediately surrounded, questioned and solicited by all to disclose the mystery of his visit. She resisted at first, but soon, becoming exasperated, she said: "What does he want? You really want to know what he wants? He wants to sleep with me."

Everybody was choked for words, and indignation was

rife. Cornudet broke his glass, so violently did he bring his fist down upon the table. There was a clamor of censure against this ignoble soldier, a blast of anger, a union of all for resistance, as if a demand had been made on each one of the party for the sacrifice exacted of her. The count declared with disgust that those people conducted themselves after the fashion of the ancient barbarians. The women, especially, showed to Ball-of-Fat a most energetic and tender commiseration. The good sisters, who only showed themselves at mealtime, lowered their heads and said nothing.

They all dined, nevertheless, when the first furore had abated. But there was little conversation; they were thinking.

The ladies retired early, and the men, all smoking, organized a game at cards to which M. Follenvie was invited, as they intended to put a few casual questions to him on the subject of conquering the resistance of this officer. But he thought of nothing but the cards and, without listening or answering, would keep repeating: "To the game sirs, to the game." His attention was so taken that he even forgot to expectorate, which must have put him some points to the good with the organ in his breast. His whistling lungs ran the whole asthmatic scale, from deep, profound tones to the sharp rustiness of a young cock essaying to crow.

He even refused to retire when his wife, who had fallen asleep previously, came to look for him. She went away alone, for she was an "early bird," always up with the sun, while her husband was a "night owl," always ready to pass the night with his friends. He cried out to her: "Leave my creamed chicken before the fire!" and then went on with his game. When they saw that they could get nothing from him they declared that it was time to stop, and each sought his bed.

They all rose rather early the next day, with an undefined hope of getting away, which desire the terror of passing another day in that horrible inn greatly increased.

Alas! the horses remained in the stable and the driver was invisible. For want of better employment they went out and walked around the carriage.

The breakfast was very doleful, and it became apparent that a coldness had arisen toward Ball-of-Fat and that the night, which brings counsel, had slightly modified their judgments. They almost wished now that the Prussian had secretly found this girl, in order to give her companions a pleasant surprise in the morning. What could be more simple? Besides, who would know anything about it? She could save appearances by telling the officer that she took pity on their distress. To her it would make so little difference!

No one had avowed these thoughts yet.

In the afternoon, as they were almost perishing from ennui, the count proposed that they take a walk around the village. Each wrapped up warmly and the little party set out, with the exception of Cornuder who preferred to remain near the fire, and the good sisters, who passed their time in the church or at the curate's.

The cold, growing more intense every day, cruelly pinched their noses and ears; their feet became so numb that each step was torture; and when they came to a field it seemed to them frightfully sad under this limitless white, so that everybody returned immediately, with hearts hard pressed and souls congealed.

The four women walked ahead, the three gentlemen followed just behind. Loiseau, who understood the situation, asked suddenly if they thought that girl there was going to keep them long in such a place as this. The count, always courteous, said that they could not exact from a woman a sacrifice so hard, unless it should come of her own will. M. Carré-Lamadon remarked that if the French made their return through Dieppe, as they were likely to, a battle would surely take place at Tôtes. This reflection made the two others anxious.

"If we could only get away on foot," said Loiseau.

The count shrugged his shoulders. "How can we think of it in this snow and with our wives?" he said. "And then we should be pursued and caught in ten minutes and led back prisoners at the mercy of these soldiers."

It was true, and they were silent.

The ladies talked of their clothes, but a certain constraint seemed to disunite them. Suddenly at the end of the street the officer appeared. His tall wasp-like figure in uniform was outlined upon the horizon formed by the snow, and he was marching with knees apart, a gait particularly military, which is affected that they may not spot their carefully blackened boots.

He bowed in passing near the ladies and looked disdainfully at the men, who preserved their dignity by not seeing him, except Loiseau, who made a motion toward raising his hat.

Ball-of-Fat reddened to the ears, and the three married women resented the great humiliation of being thus met by this soldier in the company of this girl whom he had treated so cavalierly.

But they spoke of him, of his figure and his face. Mme Carre-Lamadon, who had known many officers and considered hereself a connoisseur of them, found this one not at all bad; she regretted even that he was not French, because he would make such a pretty hussar, one all the women would rave over.

Again in the house, no one knew what to do. Some sharp words, even, were said about things very insignificant. The dinner was silent, and almost immediately after it each one went to his room to kill time in sleep.

They descended the next morning with weary faces and exasperated hearts. The women scarcely spoke to Ball-of-Fat.

A bell began to ring. It was for a baptism. The fat girl had a child being brought up among the peasants of Yvetot. She had not seen it for a year or thought of it; but now the idea of a child being baptized threw into her heart a sudden and violent tenderness for her own, and she strongly wished to be present at the ceremony.

As soon as she was gone everybody looked at each other, then pulled their chairs together, for they thought that finally something should be decided upon. Loiseau had an inspiration: It was to hold Ball-of-Fat alone and let the others go.

M. Follenvie was charged with the commission but he returned almost immediately, for the German, who understood human nature, had put him out. He pretended that he would retain everybody so long as his desire was not satisfied.

Then the commonplace nature of Mme Loiseau burst out with:

"Well, we are not going to stay here to die of old age. Since it is the trade of this creature to accommodate herself to all kinds, I fail to see how she has the right to refuse one more than another. I can tell you she has received all she could find in Rouen, even the coachmen! Yes, madame, the prefect's coachman! I know him very well, for he bought his wine at our house. And to think that today we should be drawn into this embarrassment by this affected woman, this minx! For my part, I find that this officer conducts himself very well. He has perhaps suffered privations for a long time, and doubtless he would have preferred us three; but no, he is contented with common property. He respects married women. And we must remember too that he is master. He has only to say 'I wish,' and he could take us by force with his soldiers."

The two women had a cold shiver. Pretty Mme Carré-Lamadon's eyes grew brilliant and she became a little pale, as if she saw herself already taken by force by the officer.

The men met and discussed the situation. Loiseau, furious, was for delivering "the wretch" bound hand and foot to the enemy. But the count, descended through three generations of ambassadors and endowed with the temperament of a diplomatist, was the advocate of ingenuity.

"It is best to decide upon something," said he. Then they conspired.

The women kept together, the tone of their voices was lowered, each gave advice and the discussion was general. Everything was very harmonious. The ladies, especially, found delicate shades and charming subtleties of expression for saying the most unusual things. A stranger would have understood nothing, so great was the precaution of language observed. But the light edge of modesty with which every woman of the world is barbed only covers the surface; they blossom out in a scandalous adventure of this kind, being deeply amused and feeling themselves in their element, mixing love with sensuality as a greedy cook prepares supper for his master.

Even gaiety returned, so funny did the whole story seem to them at last. The count found some of the jokes a little off color, but they were so well told that he was forced to smile. In his turn Loiseau came out with some still bolder tales, and yet nobody was wounded. The brutal thought expressed by his wife dominated all minds: "Since it is her trade, why should she refuse this one more than another?" The genteel Mme Carré-Lamadon seemed to think that in her place she would refuse this one less than some others.

They prepared the blockade at length, as if they were about to surround a fortress. Each took some role to play, some arguments he would bring to bear, some maneuvers that he would endeavor to put into execution. They decided on the plan of attack, the ruse to employ, the surprise of assault that should force this living citadel to receive the enemy in her room.

Cornudet remained apart from the rest and was a stranger to the whole affair.

So entirely were their minds distracted that they did not hear Ball-of-Fat enter. The count uttered a light "Ssh!" which turned all eyes in her direction. There she was. The abrupt silence and a certain embarrassment hindered them from speaking to her at first. The countess, more accustomed to the duplicity of society than the others, finally inquired:

"Was it very amusing, that baptism?"

The fat girl, filled with emotion, told them all about it: the faces, the attitudes and even the appearance of the church. She added: "It is good to pray sometimes."

And up to the time for luncheon these ladies continued to be amiable toward her in order to increase her docility and her confidence in their counsel. At the table they commenced the approach. This was in the shape of a vague conversation upon devotion. They cited ancient examples: Judith and Holophernes, then, whithout reason, Lucrece and Sextus, and Cleopatra obliging all the generals of the enemy to pass by her couch and reducing them in servility to slaves. Then they brought out a fantastic story, hatched in the imagination of these ignorant millionaires, when the women of Rome went to Capua for the purpose of lulling Hannibal to sleep in their arms and his lieutenants and phalanxes of mercenaries as well. They cited all the women who have been taken by conquering armies, making a battlefield of their bodies, making them also a weapon and a means of success; and all those hideous and detestable beings who have conquered by their heroic caresses and sacrificed their chastity to vengeance or a beloved cause. They even spoke in veiled terms of that great English family which allowed one of its women to be inoculated with a horrible and contagious disease in order to transmit it to Bonaparte, who was miraculously saved by a sudden illness at the hour of the fatal rendezvous.

And all this was related in an agreeable temperate fashion, except as it was enlivened by the enthusiasm deemed proper to excite emulation.

One might finally have believed that the sole duty of woman here below was a sacrifice of her person and a continual abandonment to soldierly caprices.

The two good sisters seemed not to hear, lost as they were in profound thought. Ball-of-Fat said nothing.

During the whole afternoon they let her reflect. But in the place of calling her "Madame," as they had up to this time, they simply called her "Mademoiselle" without knowing exactly why, as if they had a desire to put her down a degree in their esteem, which she had taken by storm, and make her feel her shameful situation.

The moment supper was served M. Follenvie appeared with his old phrase: "The Prussian officer orders me to ask if Miss Elizabeth Rousset has yet changed her mind."

Ball-of-Fat responded dryly: "No sir."

But at dinner the coalition weakened. Loiseau made three unhappy remarks. Each one beat his wits for new examples but found nothing; then the countess, without premeditation, perhaps feeling some vague need of rendering homage to religion, asked the elder of the good sisters to tell them some great deeds in the lives of the saints. It appeared that many of their acts would have been considered crimes in our eyes, but the Church gave absolution of them readily, since they were done for the glory of God or for the good of all. It was a powerful argument; the countess made the most of it.

Thus it may be by one of those tacit understandings, or the veiled complacency in which anyone who wears the ecclesiastical garb excels, it may be simply from the effect of a happy unintelligence, a helpful stupidity, but in fact the religious sister lent a formidable support to the conspiracy. They had thought her timid, but she showed herself courageous, verbose, even violent. She was not troubled by the chatter of the casuist; her doctrine seemed a bar of iron; her faith never hesitated; her conscience had no scruples. She found the scarifice of Abraham perfectly simple, for she would immediately kill father or mother on an order from on high. And nothing, in her opinion, could displease the Lord if the intention was laudable. The countess put to use the authority of her unwitting accomplice and added to it the edifying paraphrase and axiom of Jesuit morals: "The need justifies the means."

Then she asked her: "Then, my sister, do you think that God accepts intentions and pardons the deed when the motive is pure?"

"Who could doubt it, madame? An action blamable in itself often becomes meritorious by the thought it springs from."

And they continued thus, unraveling the will of God, foreseeing his decisions, making themselves interested in things that, in truth, they would never think of noticing. All this was guarded, skillful, discreet. But each word of the saintly sister in a cap helped to break down the resistance of the unworthy courtesan. Then the conversation changed a little, the woman of the chaplet speaking of the houses of her order, of her Superior, of herself, of her dainty neighbor, the dear sister Saint Nicephore. They had been called to the hospitals of Havre to care for the hundreds of soldiers stricken with smallpox. They depicted these miserable creatures, giving details of the malady. And while they were stopped, en route, by the caprice of this Prussian officer, a great number of Frenchmen might die whom perhaps they could have saved! It was a specialty with her, caring for soldiers. She had been in Crimea, in Italy, in Austria, and in telling of her campaigns she revealed herself as one of those religious aids to drums and trumpets who seem made to follow camps, pick up the wounded in the thick of battle and, better than an officer, subdue with a word great bands of undisciplined recruits. A true good sister of the rataplan, whose ravaged face, marked with innumerable scars appeared the image of the devastation of war.

No one could speak after her, so excellent seemed the effect of her words.

As soon as the repast was ended they quickly went up to their rooms, with the purpose of not coming down the next day until late in the morning.

The luncheon was quiet. They had given the grain of seed time to germinate and bear fruit. The countess proposed that they take a walk in the afternoon. The count, being agreeably inclined, gave an arm to Ball-of-Fat and walked behind the others with her. He talked to her in a familiar, paternal tone, a little disdainful, after the manner of men having girls in their employ, calling her "my dear child," from the height of his social position, of his undisputed honor. He reached the vital part of the question at once:

"Then you prefer to leave us here, exposed to the violences which follow a defeat, rather than consent to a favor which you have so often given in your life?"

Ball-of-Fat answered nothing.

Then he tried to reach her through gentleness, reason, and then the sentiments. He knew how to remain "the count," even while showing himself gallant or complimentary or very amiable if it became necessary. He exalted the service that she would render them and spoke of his appreciation, then suddenly became gaily familiar and said:

"And you know, my dear, it would be something for him to boast of that he had known a pretty girl; something it is difficult to find in his country."

Ball-of-Fat did not answer but joined the rest of the party. As soon as they entered the house she went to her room and did not appear again. The disquiet was extreme. What were they to do? If she continued to resist, what an embarrassment!

The dinner hour struck. They waited in vain. M.

Follenvie finally entered and said that Miss Rousset was indisposed and would not be at the table. Everybody pricked up his ears. The count went to the innkeeper and said in a low voice:

"Is he in there?"

"Yes."

For convenience he said nothing to his companions but made a slight sign with his head. Immediately a great sigh of relief went up from every breast and a light appeared in their faces. Loiseau cried out:

"Holy Christopher! *I* pay for the champagne, if there is any to be found in the establishment." And Mme Loiseau was pained to see the proprietor return with four quart bottles in his hands.

Each one had suddenly become communicative and buoyant. A wanton joy filled their hearts. The count suddenly perceived that Mme Carré-Lamadon was charming, the manufacturer paid compliments to the countess. The conversation was lively, gay, full of touches.

Suddenly Loiseau, with anxious face and hand upraised, called out: "Silence!" Everybody was silent, surprised, already frightened. Then he listened intently and said: "S-s-sh!" his two eyes and his hands raised toward the ceiling, listening, and then continuing in his natural voice: "All right! All goes well!"

They failed to comprehend at first, but soon all laughed. At the end of a quarter of an hour he began the same farce again, renewing it occasionally during the whole afternoon. And he pretended to call to someone in the story above, giving him advice in a double meaning, drawn from the fountainhead—the mind of a commercial traveler. For some moments he would assume a sad air, breathing in a whisper: "Poor girl!" Then he would murmur between his teeth, with an appearance of rage: "Ugh! That scamp of a Prussian." Sometimes, at a moment when no more was thought about it, he would say in an affected voice, many times over: "Enough! enough!" and add, as if speaking to himself: "If we could only see her again; it isn't necessary that he should kill her, the wretch!"

Although these jokes were in deplorable taste they amused all and wounded no one, for indignation, like other things, depends upon its surroundings, and the atmosphere, which had been gradually created around them was charged with sensual thoughts.

At the dessert the women themselves made some delicate and discreet allusions. Their eyes glistened; they had drunk much. The count, who preserved even in his flights his grand appearance of gravity, made a comparison, much relished, upon the subject of those wintering at the Pole, and the joy of shipwrecked sailors who saw an opening toward the south.

Loiseau suddenly arose, a glass of champagne in his hand, and said: "I drink to our deliverance." Everybody was on his feet; they shouted in agreement. Even the two good sisters consented to touch their lips to the froth of the wine which they had never before tasted. They declared that it tasted like charged lemonade, only much nicer.

Loiseau resumed: "It is unfortunate that we have no piano, for we might make up a quadrille."

Cornudet had not said a word nor made a gesture; he appeared plunged in very grave thoughts and made sometimes a furious motion, so that his great beard seemed to wish to free itself. Finally, toward midnight, as they were separating, Loiseau, who was staggering, touched him suddenly on the stomach and said to him in a stammer: "You are not very funny this evening; you have said nothing, citizen!" Then Cornudet raised his head brusquely and, casting a brilliant, terrible glance around the company, said: "I tell you all that you have been guilty of infamy!" He rose, went to the door and again repeated: "Infamy, I say!" and disappeared.

This made a coldness at first. Loiseau, interlocutor, was stupefied; but he recovered immediately and laughed heartily as he said: "He is very green, my friends. He is very green." And then, as they did not comprehend, he told them about the "mysteries of the corridor." Then there was a return of gaiety. The women behaved like lunatics. The count and M. Carré-Lamadon wept from the force of their laughter. They could not believe it.

"How is that? Are you sure?"

"I tell you I saw it."

"And she refused—"

"Yes, because the Prussian officer was in the next room."

"Impossible!"

"I swear it!"

The count was stifled with laughter. The industrial gentleman held his sides with both hands. Loiseau continued:

"And now you understand why he saw nothing funny this evening! No, nothing at all!" And the three started out half ill, suffocated.

They separated. But Mme Loiseau, who was of a spiteful nature, remarked to her husband as they were getting into bed that "that grisette" of a little Carré-Lamadon was yellow with envy all the evening. "You know," she continued, "how some women will take to a uniform, whether it be French or Prussian. It is all the same to them. Oh, what a pity!"

And all night, in the darkness of the corridor, there were to be heard light noises like whisperings and walking in bare feet and imperceptible creakings. They did not go to sleep until late, that is sure, for there were threads of light shining under the doors for a long time. The champagne had its effect; they say it troubles sleep.

The next day a clear winter's sun made the snow very brilliant. The diligence, already harnessed, waited before the door while an army of white pigeons, in their thick plumage, with rose-colored eyes with a black spot in the center, walked up and down gravely among the legs of the six horses, seeking their livelihood in the manure there scattered.

The driver, enveloped in his sheepskin, had a lighted pipe under the seat, and all the travelers, radiant, were rapidly packing some provisions for the rest of the journey. They were only waiting for Ball-of-Fat. Finally she appeared.

She seemed a little troubled, ashamed. And she advanced timidly toward her companions, who all, with one motion, turned as if they had not seen her. The count, with dignity, took the arm of his wife and removed her from this impure contact.

The fat girl stopped, half stupefied; then, plucking up courage, she approached the manufacturer's wife with "Good morning, madame," humbly murmured. The lady made a slight bow of the head which she accompanied with a look of outraged virtue. Everybody seemed busy and kept themselves as far from her as if she had had some infectious disease in her skirts. Then they hurried into the carriage, where she came last, alone, and where she took the place she had occupied during the first part of the journey.

They seemed not to see her or know her; although Mme Loiseau, looking at her from afar, said to her husband in a half tone: "Happily, I don't have to sit beside her."

The heavy carriage began to move, and the remainder of the journey commenced. No one spoke at first. Ball-of-Fat dared not raise her eyes. She felt indignant toward all her neighbors and at the same time humiliated at having yielded to the foul kisses of this Prussian into whose arms they had hypocritically thrown her.

Then the countess, turning toward Mme Carré-Lamadon, broke the difficult silence:

"I believe you know Madame d'Etrelles?"

"Yes, she is one of my friends."

"What a charming woman!"

"Delightful! A very gentle nature and well educated besides; then she is an artist to the tips of her fingers, sings beautifully and draws to perfection."

The manufacturer chatted with the count, and in the midst of the rattling of the glass an occasional word escaped such as "coupon—premium—limit—expiration."

Loiseau, who had pilfered the old pack of cards from the inn, greasy through five years of contact with tables badly cleaned, began a game of bezique with his wife.

The good sisters took from their belt the long rosary which hung there, made together the sign of the cross and suddenly began to move their lip in a lively murmur, as if they were going through the whole of the "Oremus." And from time to time they kissed a medal, made the sign anew, then recommenced their muttering, which was rapid and continued.

Cornudet sat motionless, thinking.

At the end of three hours on the way, Loiseau put up the cards and said: "I am hungry."

His wife drew out a package from whence she brought a piece of cold veal. She cut it evenly in thin pieces and they both began to eat.

"Suppose we do the same," said the countess.

They consented to it and she undid the provisions prepared for the two couples. It was in one of those dishes whose lid is decorated with a china hare to signify that a *pâté* of hare is inside, a succulent dish of pork, where white rivers of lard cross the brown flesh of the game, mixed wrapped in a piece of newspaper, preserved the imprint "divers things" upon the unctuous plate.

The two good sisters unrolled a big sausage which smelled of garlic, and Cornudet plunged his two hands into the vast pockets of his overcoat at the same time and drew out four hard eggs and a piece of bread. He removed the shells and threw them in the straw under his feet; then he began to eat the eggs, letting fall on his vast beard some bits of clear yellow which looked like stars caught there.

Ball-of-Fat, in the haste and distraction of her rising, had not thought of anything; and she looked at them exasperated, suffocating with rage at all of them eating so placidly. A tumultuous anger swept over her at first, and she opened her mouth to cry out at them, to hurl at them a flood of injury which mounted to her lips; but she could not speak, her exasperation strangled her.

No one looked at her or thought of her. She felt herself drowned in the scorn of these honest scoundrels who had first sacrificed her and then rejected her, like some improper or useless article. She thought of her great basketful of good things they had greedily devoured, of her two chickens shining with jelly, of her *pâtés,* her pears and the four bottles of Bordeaux, and her fury suddenly falling, as a cord drawn too tightly breaks, she felt ready to weep. She made terrible efforts to prevent it, making ugly faces, swallowing her sobs as children do; but the tears came and themselves from the rest, rolled slowly down like little streams of water that filter through rock and, falling regularly, rebounded upon her breast. She sits erect, her eyes fixed, her face rigid and pale, hoping that no one will notice her.

But the countess perceived her and tells her husband by a sign. He shrugs his shoulders, as much as to say:

"What would you have me do? It is not my fault."

Mme Loiseau indulged in a mute laugh of triumph and murmured:

"She weeps for shame."

The two good sisters began to pray again, after having wrapped in a paper the remainder of their sausage.

Then Cornudet, who was digesting his eggs, extended his legs to the seat opposite, crossed them, folded his arms, smiled like a man who is watching a good farce and began to whistle the "Marseillaise."

All faces grew dark. The popular song assuredly did not please his neighbors. They became nervous and agitated, having an appearance of wishing to howl, like dogs when they hear a barbrous organ. He perceived this but did not stop. Sometimes he would hum the words:

> *"Sacred love of country*
> *Help, sustain th' avenging arm;*
> *Liberty, sweet Liberty,*
> *Even fight, with no alarm."*

They traveled fast, the snow being harder. But as far as Dieppe, during the long sad hours of the journey, across the jolts in the road, through the falling night, in the profound darkness of the carriage, he continued his vengeful, monotonous whistling with a ferocious obstinacy, constraining his neighbors to follow the song from one end to the other and to recall the words that belonged to each measure.

And Ball-of-Fat wept continually, and sometimes a sob, which she was not able to restrain, echoed between the two rows of people in the shadows.

A LITTLE WALK

When father Leras, bookkeeper with Messrs Labuze and Company, went out of the store, he stood for some minutes, dazzled by the brilliancy of the setting sun.

He had toiled all day under the yellow light of the gas jet at the end of the rear shop, on the court which was as narrow and deep as a well. The little room in which for forty years he had spent his days was so dark that even in the middle of summer they could hardly dispense with the gas from eleven to three o'clock.

It was always cold and damp there, and the emanations from that sort of hole on which the window looked came into the gloomy room, filling it with an odor moldy and sewerlike.

M. Leras for forty years arrived at eight o'clock in the morning at this prison, and he remained till seven at night, bent over his books, writing with the faithfulness of a good employee.

He now earned three thousand francs per year, having begun with fifteen hundred francs. He had remained unmarried, his means not permitting him to take a wife. And never having enjoyed anything, he did not desire much. From time to time, nevertheless, weary of his monotonous and continuous work, he made a platonic vow:

"Cristi, if I had five thousand livres' income I would enjoy life!"

He had never enjoyed life, never having had more than

his monthly salary.

His existence passed without events, without emotion and almost without hopes. The faculty of dreaming, which everyone has in him, had never developed in the mediocrity of his ambitions.

He had entered the employ of Messrs Labuze and Company at twenty-one years of age. And he had never left it.

In 1856 he had lost his father, then his mother in 1859. And since then he had experienced nothing but a removal, his landlord having wanted to raise his rent.

Every day his morning alarm, exactly at six o'clock, made him jump out of bed by its fearful racket.

Twice however, this machine had run down, in 1866 and in 1874, without his ever knowing why.

He dressed, made his bed, swept his room, dusted his armchair and the top of his commode. All these duties required an hour and a half.

Then he went out, bought a roll at the Lahure bakery, which had had a dozen different proprietors without losing its name, and he set out for the office, eating the bread on the way.

His whole existence was thus accomplished in the narrow dark office which was adorned with the same wallpaper. He had entered the employ young, an assistant to M. Burment and with the desire of taking his place.

He had taken his place and expected nothing further.

All that harvest of memories which other men make during their lives, the unforeseen events, the sweet or tragic love affairs, the adventurous journeys, all the hazards of a free existence, had been strange to him.

The days, the weeks, the months, the seasons, the years, were all alike. At the same hour every day he rose, left the house, arrived at the office, took his luncheon, went away, dined and retired without ever having interrupted the monotony of the same acts, the same deeds and the same thoughts.

Formerly he looked at his blond mustache and curly hair in the little round glass left by his predecessor. He now looked every morning, before going out, at his white mustache and his bald head in the same glass. Forty years had flown, long and rapid, empty as a day of sorrow and like the long hours of a bad night–forty years, of which nothing remained, not even a memory, not even a misfortune, since the death of his parents, nothing.

That day M. Leras stood dazzled at the street door by the brilliancy of the setting sun, and instead of returning to his house he had the idea of taking a little walk before dinner, something which he did four or five times a year.

He reached the boulevard, where many people were passing under the budding trees. It was an evening in springtime, one of those first soft, warm evenings which stir the heart with the intoxication of life.

M. Leras walked along with his mincing old man's step, with a gaiety in his eye, happy with the unusual joy and the mildness of the air.

He reached the Champs Elysées and proceeded, reanimated by the odors of youth which filled the breeze.

The whole sky glowed, and the Triumphal Arch stood with its dark mass against the shining horizon, like a giant struggling in a conflagration. When he had nearly reached the stupendous monument the old bookkeeper felt hungry and went into a wineshop to dine.

They served him in front of the shop, on the sidewalk, a sheep's-foot stew, a salad and some asparagus, and M. Leras made the best dinner he had made in a long while.

He washed down his Brie cheese with a small bottle of good Bordeaux; he drank a cup of coffee, which seldom occurred to him, and finally a tiny glass of brandy.

When he had paid he felt quite lively and brisk, even a little perturbed. He said: "I will continue my walk as far as the entrance to the Bois de Boulogne. It will do me good."

He started. An old air which one of his neighbors used to sing long ago came to his mind:

> *When the park grows green and gay*
> *Then doth my brave lover say,*
> *"Come with me, my sweet and fair,*
> *To get a breath of air."*

He hummed it continually, beginning it over again and again. Night had fallen upon Paris, a night without wind, a night of sweet calm. M. Leras followed the Avenue de Bois de Boulogne and watched the cabs pass. They came with their bright lamps, one after another, giving a fleeting glimpse of a couple embracing, the woman in light-colored dress and the man clad in black.

It was a long procession of lovers, driving under the starry and sultry sky. They kept arriving continually. They passed, reclining in the carriages, silent, pressed to one another, lost in the hallucination, the emotion of desire, in the excitement of the approaching culmination. The warm darkness seemed full of floating kisses. A sensation of tenderness made the air languishing and stifling. All these embracing people, all these persons intoxicated with the same intention, the same thought, caused a fever around them. All these carriages full of caresses diffused as they passed, as it were, a subtle and disturbing emanation.

M. Leras, a little wearied finally by walking, took a

seat on a bench watch these carriages loaded with love. And almost immediately a woman came near to him and took her place at his side.

"Good evening, my little man," she said.

He did not reply. She continued:

"Don't you want a sweetheart?"

"You are mistaken, madame."

And she took his arm.

"Come, don't be a fool; listen—"

He had risen and gone away, his heart oppressed.

A hundred steps farther on another woman approached him.

"Won't you sit down a moment with me, my fine boy?"

He said to her:

"Why do you lead such a life?"

"Name of God, it isn't always for my pleasure."

He continued in a soft voice:

"Then what compels you?"

She: "Must live, you know." And she went away, singing.

M. Leras stood, astonished. Other women passed near him, similarly accosting him. It seemed to him that something dark was setting upon his head, something heartbreaking. And he seated himself again upon a bench. The carriages kept hurrying by.

"Better not to have come here," he thought. "I am all unsettled."

He began to think on all this love, venal or passionate, on all these kisses bought or free, which streamed before him.

Love, he hardly knew what it meant. He never had had more than two or three sweethearts in all his life, his means not permitting. And he thought of that life which he had led, so different from the life of all, his life so dark, so dull, so flat, so empty.

There are beings who truly never have any luck. And all at once, as if a thick veil had been lifted, he perceived the misery, the infinite, monotonous misery of his existence: the past misery, the present misery, the future misery, the last days like the first, with nothing before him, nothing behind him, nothing around him, nothing in his heart, nothing anywhere.

The carriages kept passing. He saw appearing and disappearing in the rapid flight of the open *fiacre* the two beings, silent and embracing. It seemed to him that the whole of humanity was filing before him, intoxicated with joy, with pleasure, with happiness. And he was alone looking on at it, all alone. He would be still alone tomorrow, alone always, alone as no one else is alone.

He rose, took a few steps, and suddenly fatigued, as if he has walked for many miles, he sat down on the next bench.

What was awaiting him? What did he hope for? Nothing. He thought how good it must be when a man is old to find, on getting home, little prattling children there. To grow old is sweet when a person is surrounded by those beings who owe him their life, who love him, who caress him, saying those charming, foolish words which warm the heart and console him for everything.

And thinking of his empty room, neat and sad, where never a person entered but himself, a feeling of distress overwhelmed his soul. It seemed to him that room was more lamentable even than his little office.

No one came to it; no one spoke in it. It was dead, silent, without the echo of a human voice. One would say that the walls had something of the people who lived within, something of their look, their face, their words.

The houses inhabited by happy families are more gay than the habitations of the wretched. His room was empty of memories, like his life, and the thought of going back into that room all alone, of sleeping in his bed, of doing over again all his actions and all his duties of evening terrified him. And as if to put himself farther away from this gloomy lodging and from the moment when he would have to return to it, he rose and, finding all at once the first pathway of the park, he entered a clump of woods to sit upon the grass.

He heard round about him, above him, everywhere, a confused sound, immense and countinuous, made of innumerable different voices, near and far, a vague and enormous palpiation of life—the breath of Paris respiring like some colossal being.

The sun already high cast a flood of light upon the Bois de Boulogne. Some carriages began to circulate, and the horseback riders gaily arrived.

A couple were going at a walk through a lonely bridle path.

Suddenly the young woman, raising her eyes, perceived something brown among the branches; she raised her hand, astonished and disturbed.

"Look–what is that?"

Then uttering a scream, she let herself fall into the arms of the companion, who placed her on the ground.

The guards, quickly summoned, unfastened an old man hanging to a branch by his braces.

It was agreed that the deceased had hanged himself the evening before.

The papers found upon him disclosed the fact that he

was the bookkeeper for Messrs Labuze and Company and that his name was Leras.

They attributed his death to suicide, for which the cause could not be determined. Perhaps a sudden attack of madness.

THE SUBSTITUTE

"Madame Bonderoi?"
"Yes, Madame, Bonderoi."
"Impossible."
"I tell you it is."
"Madame Bonderoi, the old lady in a lace cap, the devout, the holy, the honorable Madame Bonderoi, whose little false curls look as if they were glued round her head?"
"That is the very woman."
"Oh, come, you must be mad."
"I swear to you that it is Madame Bonderoi."
"Then please give me the details."
"Here they are: During the life of Monsieur Bonderoi, the lawyer, people said that she utilized his clerks for her own particular service. She is one of those respectable middle-class women, with secret vices and inflexible principles, of whom there are so many. She liked good-looking young fellows, and I should like to know what is more natural than that? Do not we all like pretty girls?

"As soon as old Bonderoi was dead his widow began to live the peaceful and irreproachable life of a woman with a fair, fixed income. She went to church assiduously and spoke evil of her neighbors but gave no chance to anyone to speak ill of her, and when she grew old she became the little wizened, sour-faced, mischievous woman whom you know. Well, this adventure, which you would scarcely believe, happened last Friday.

"My friend, Jean d'Anglemare, is, as you know, a captain in a dragoon regiment which is quartered in the barracks in the Rue de la Rivette. When he got to his quarter the other morning he found that two men of his squadron had had a terrible quarrel. The duel took place between them. After the duel they became reconciled, and when their officer questioned them they told him what their quarrel had been about. They had fought on Madame Bonderoi's account."

"Oh!"

"Yes, my dear fellow, about Madame Bonderoi. But I will let Trooper Siballe speak":

"'This is how it was, Captain. About a year and a half ago I was lounging about the barrack yard between six and seven o'clock in the evening, when a woman came up and spoke to me and said, just as if she had been asking her way: "Soldier, would you like to earn ten francs a week honestly?" Of course I told her that I should, and so she said: "Come and see me at twelve o'clock tomorrow morning. I am Madame Bonderoi, and my address is number 6, Rue de la Tranchée."

"'"You may rely upon my being there, madame." And then she went away, looking very pleased, and added: "I am very much obliged to you, soldier."

"'"I am obliged to you, madame," I replied. But I plagued my head about the matter until the time came, all the same.

"'At twelve o'clock exactly I rang the bell, and she let me in herself. She had a lot of ribbons on her head.

"'"We must make haste," she said, "as my servant might come in."

"'"I am quite willing to make haste," I replied, "but what am I to do?"

"'But she only laughed and replied: "Don't you understand, you great stupid?"

"'I was no nearer her meaning, I give you my word of honor, Captain, but she came and sat down by me and said:

"'"If you mention this to anyone I will have you put in prison, so swear that you will never open your lips about it."

"'I swore whatever she liked, though I did not at all understand what she meant. My forehead was covered with perspiration, so I took my pocket handkerchief out of my helmet. She took it and wiped my brow with it; then she kissed me and whispered: "Then you will?"

"'"I will do anything you like, madame," I replied, "as that is what I came for."

"'Then she made herself clearly understood by her actions, and when I saw what it was, I put my helmet on a chair and showed her that in the dragoons a man never retires, Captain.

"'Not that I cared much about it, for she was certainly not in her prime, but it is no good being too particular in such a matter, as francs are scarce, and then I have relations whom I like to help. I said to myself: "There will be five francs for my father, out of that."

"'When I had finished my allotted task, Captain, I got ready to go, though she wanted me to stop longer, but I said to her:

"'"To everyone their due, madame. A small glass of brandy costs two sous, and two glasses cost four."

"'She understood my meaning and put a gold ten-franc piece into my hand. I do not like that coin. It is so small that if your pockets are not very well made and come at all unsewn one is apt to find it in one's boots or not to find it at all, and so, while I was looking at it, she was looking at me. She got red in the face, as she had misunderstood my looks, and said: "Is not that enough?"

"'"I did not mean that, madame," I replied, "but if it is all the same to you, I would rather have two five-franc pieces." And she gave them to me, and I took my leave.

"'This has bean going on for a year and a half, Captain. I go every Tuesday evening, when you give me leave to go out of barracks; she prefers that, as her servant has gone to bed then, but last week I was not well and I had to go into the infirmary. When Tuesday came I could not get out, and I was very vexed because of the ten francs which I had been receiving every week, and I said to myself:

"'"If anybody goes there I shall be done for, and she will be sure to take an artilleryman," and that made me angry. So I sent for Paumelle, who comes from my part of the country, and I told him how matters stood:

"'"There will be five francs for you and five for me," I said. He agreed and went, as I had given him full instructions. She opened the door as soon as he knocked and let him in, and as she did not look at his face, she did not perceive that it was not I, for you know, Captain, one dragoon is very like another with a helmet on.

"'Suddenly, however, she noticed the change and she asked angrily: "Who are you? What do you want? I do not know you."

"'Then Paumelle explained matters; he told her that I was not well and that I had sent him as my substitute, so she looked at him, made him also swear to keep the matter secret, and then she accepted him, as you may suppose, for Paumelle is not a bad-looking fellow either. But when he came back, Captain, he would not give me my five francs. If they had been for myself I should not have said a word, but they were for my father, and on that score I would stand no nonsense and said to him:

"'"You are not particular in what you do, for a dragoon, you are a discredit to your uniform."

"'He raised his fist, Captain, saying that fatigue duty like that was worth double. Of course everybody has his own ideas, and he ought not to have accepted it. You know the rest.'

"Captain d'Anglemare laughed until he cried as he told me the story, but he also made me promise to keep the matter a secret, just as he had promised the two soldiers. So above all do not betray me, but promise me to keep it to yourself."

"Oh! You may be quite easy about that. But how was it all arranged in the end?"

"How? It is a joke in a thousand! Mother Bonderoi keeps her two dragoons and reserves his own particular day for each of them, and in that way everybody is satisfied."

"Oh! That is capital! Really capital!"

"And he can send his old father and mother the money as usual, and thus morality is satisfied."

A DUEL

THE WAR WAS OVER. The Germans occupied France. The country was panting like a wrestler lying under the knee of his successful opponent.

The first trains from Paris, after the city's long agony of famine and despair, were making their way to the new frontiers, slowly passing through the country districts and the villages. The passengers gazed through the windows at the ravaged fields and burned hamlets. Prussian soldiers, in their black hamlets with brass spikes, were smoking their pipes on horseback or sitting on chairs in front of the houses which were still left standing. Others were working or talking just as if they were members of the families. As you passed through the different towns you saw entire regiments drilling in the squares, and in spite of the rumble of the carriage wheels you could, every moment, hear the hoarse words of command.

M. Dubuis, who during the entire siege had served as one of he National Guard in Paris, was going to join his wife and daughter, whom he had prudently sent away to Switzerland before the invasion.

Famine and hardship had not diminished the big paunch so characteristic of the rich, peace-loving merchant. He had gone through the terrible events of the past year with sorrowful resignation and bitter complaints at the savagery of men. Now that he was journeying to the frontier at the close of the war he saw the Prussians for the first time, although he had done duty at the ramparts and stanchly mounted guard on cold nights.

He stared with mingled fear and anger at those bearded armed men installed all over French soil as if in their own homes, and he felt in his soul a kind of fever of impotent patriotism even while he yielded to that other instinct of discretion and self-preservation which never leaves us. In the same compartment two Englishmen, who had come to the country as sight-seers, were gazing around with looks of stolid curiosity. They were both stout also and kept chattering in their own language, sometimes referring to their guidebook and reading in loud tones the names of the places indicated.

Suddenly the train stopped at a little village station, and a Prussian officer jumped up with a great clatter of his saber on the double footboard of the railway carriage. He was tall, wore a tight-fitting uniform, and his face had a very shaggy aspect. His red hair seemed to be on fire, and his long mustache and beard, of a paler color, was stuck out on both sides of his face, which it seemed to cut in two.

The Englishmen at once began staring at him with smiles of newly awakened interest, while M. Dubuis made a show of reading a newspaper. He sat crouched in a corner, like a thief in the presence of a gendarme.

The train started again. The Englishmen went on chatting and looking out for the exact scene of different battles, and all of a sudden, as one of them stretched out his arm toward the horizon to indicate a village, the Prussian officer remarked in French, extending his long legs and lolling backward:

"We killed a dozen Frenchmen in that village and took more than a hundred prisoners."

The Englishmen, quite interested, immediately asked:

"Ha! And what is the name of this village?"

The Prussian replied:

"Pharsbourg."

He added: "We caught these French blackguards by the ears."

And he glanced toward M. Dubuis, laughing into his mustache in an insulting fashion.

The train rolled on, always passing through hamlets occupied by the victorious army. German soldiers could be seen along the roads, on the edges of fields, standing in front of gates or chatting outside cafés. They covered the soil like African locusts.

The officer said with a wave of his hand:

"If I were in command I'd take Paris, burn everything and kill everybody. No more France!"

The Englishmen, through politeness, replied simply:

"Ah yes."

He went on:

"In twenty years all Europe, all of it, will belong to us. Prussia is more than a match for all of them."

The Englishmen, getting uneasy, said nothing in answer to this. Their faces, which had become impassive, seemed made of wax behind their long whiskers. Then the Prussian officer began to laugh. And then, lolling back, he began to sneer. He sneered at the downfall of France, insulted the prostrate enemy; he sneered at Austria which had been recently conquered; he sneered at the furious but fruitless defense of the departments; he sneered at the Garde Mobile and at the useless artillery. He announced that Bismarck was going to build a city of iron with the captured cannons. And suddenly he pushed his boots against the thigh of M. Dubuis, who turned his eyes away, reddening to the roots of his hair.

The Englishmen seemed to have assumed an air of complete indifference, as if they had found themselves all at once shut up in their own island, far from the din of the world.

The officer took out his pipe and, looking fixedly at the Frenchman, said:

"You haven't got any tobacco—have you?"

M. Dubuis replied:

"No, monsieur."

The German said:

"You might go and buy some for me when the train stops next."

And he began laughing afresh as he added:

"I'll let you have the price of a drink."

The train whistled and slackened its pace. They had reached a station which had been burned down, and here there was a regular stop.

The German opened the carriage door and, catching M. Dubuis by the arm, said:

"Go and do what I told you—quick, quick!"

A Prussian detachment occupied the station. Other soldiers were looking on from behind wooden gratings. The engine was already getting up steam in order to start off again. Then M. Dubuis hurriedly jumped on the platform and, in spite of the warnings of the stationmaster, dashed into the adjoining compartment.

He was alone! He tore open his waistcoat, so rapidly did his heart beat, and, panting for breath, he wiped the perspiration off his forehead.

The train drew up at another station. And suddenly the officer appeared at the carriage door and jumped in, followed close behind by the two Englishmen, who were impelled by curiosity. The German sat facing the

Frenchman and, laughing still, said:

"You did not want to do what I asked you."

M. Dubuis replied: "No, monsieur."

The train had just left the station when the officer said:

"I'll cut off your mustache to fill my pipe with." And he put his hand toward the Frenchman's face.

The Englishmen kept staring in the same impassive fashion with fixed glances. Already the German had caught hold of the mustache and was tugging at it, when M. Dubuis, with a backstroke of his hand, threw back the officer's arm and, seizing him by the collar, flung him down on the seat. Then, excited to a pitch of fury, with his temples swollen and his eyes glaring he kept throttling the officer with one hand while with the other, clenched, he began to strike him violent blows in the face. The Prussian struggled, tried to draw his saber and to get a grip, while lying back, on his adversary. But M. Dubuis crushed him with the enormous weight of his stomach and kept hitting him without taking breath or knowing where his blows fell. Blood flowed down the face of the German, who, choking and with a rattling in his throat, spat forth his broken teeth and vainly strove to shake off this infuriated man who was killing him.

The Englishmen had got on their feet and came closer to see better. They remained standing, full of mirth and curiosity, ready to bet for or against each of the combatants.

And suddenly M. Dubuis, exhausted by his violent efforts, went and resumed his seat without uttering a word.

The Prussian did not attack him, for the savage assault had scared and terrified the officer. When he was able to breathe freely he said:

"Unless you give me satisfaction with pistols I will

kill you."

M. Dubuis replied:

"Whenever you like. I'm quite ready."

The German said:

"Here is the town of Strasbourg. I'll get two officers to be my seconds, and there will be time before the train leaves the station."

M. Dubuis, who was puffing as much as the engine, said to the Englishmen:

"Will you be my seconds?" They both answered together:

"Oh yes."

And the train stopped.

In a minute the Prussian had found two comrades who carried pistols, and they made their way toward the ramparts.

The Englishmen were continually looking at their watches, shuffling their feet and hurrying on with the preparations, uneasy lest they should be too late for the train.

M. Dubuis had never fired a pistol in his life. They made him stand twenty paces away from his enemy. He was asked:

"Are you ready?"

While he was answering "Yes, monsieur," he noticed that one of the Englishmen had opened his umbrella in order to keep off the rays of the sun.

A voice gave the word of command.

"Fire!"

M. Dubuis fired at random without minding what he was doing, and he was amazed to see the Prussian staggering in front of him, lifting up his arms and, immediately afterward, falling straight on his face. He had killed the officer.

One of the Englishmen ejaculated: "Ah!" quivering with delight, satisfied curiosity and joyous impatience. The other, who still kept his watch in his hand, hurried him in double-quick time toward the station, his fellow country-man counting their steps with his arms pressed close to his sides: "One, two! One, two!"

And all three marching abreast, they rapidly made their way to the station like three grotesque figures in a comic newspaper.

The train was on the point of starting. They sprang into their carriage. Then the Englishmen, taking off their traveling caps, waved them three times over their heads, exclaiming:

"Hip! hip! hip! hurrah!"

Then gravely, one after the other, they stretched out their right hands to M. Dubuis and then went back and sat in their own corner.

THE UMBRELLA

Mme Oreille was a very economical woman; she thoroughly knew the value of a halfpenny and possessed a whole storehouse of strict principles with regard to the multiplication of money, so that her cook found the greatest difficulty in making what the servants call their "market penny," while her husband was hardly allowed any pocket money at all. They were, however, very comfortably off and had no children. It really pained Mme Oreille to see any money spent; it was like tearing at her heartstrings when she had to take any of those nice crown pieces out of her pocket, and whenever she had to spend anything, no matter how necessary it was, she slept badly the next night.

Oreille was continually saying to his wife:

"You really might be more liberal, as we have no children and never spend our income."

"You don't know what may happen," she used to reply. "It is better to have too much than too little."

She was a little woman of about forty, very active, rather hasty, wrinkled, very neat and tidy and with a very short temper. Her husband very often used to complain of all the privations she made him endure; some of them were particularly painful to him, as they touched his vanity.

He was one of the upper clerks in the War Office and only stayed there in obedience to his wife's wish, so as to increase their income, which they did not nearly spend.

For two years he had always come to the office with

the same old patched umbrella, to the great amusement of his fellow clerks. At last he got tired of their jokes and insisted upon his wife buying him a new one. She bought one for eight francs and a half, one of those cheap things which large houses sell as an advertisement. When the others in the office saw the article, which was being sold in Paris by the thousand, they began their jokes again, and Oreille had a dreadful time of it with them. They even made a song about it, which he heard from morning till night all over the immense building.

Oreille was very angry and peremptorily told his wife to get him a new one, a good silk one, for twenty francs and to bring him the bill, so that he might see that it was all right.

She bought him one for eighteen francs and said, getting red with anger as she gave it to her husband:

"This will last you for five years at least."

Oreille felt quite triumphant and obtained a small ovation at the office with his new acquisition. When he went home in the evening his wife said to him, looking at the umberella uneasily:

"You should not leave it fastened up with the elastic; it will very likely cut the silk. You must take care of it, for I shall not buy you a new one in a hurry."

She took it, unfastened it and then remained dumfounded with astonishment and rage. In the middle of the silk there was a hole as big as a six-penny piece, as if made with the end of a cigar.

"What is that?" she screamed.

Her husband replied quietly without looking at it:

"What is it? What do you mean?"

She was choking with rage and could hardly get out a word.

"You—you—have burned—your umberlla! Why—you must be—mad! Do you wish to ruin us outright?"

He turned round hastily, as if frightened.

"What are you talking about?"

"I say that you have burned your umbrella. Just look here."

And rushing at him, as if she were going to beat him, she violently thrust the little circular burned hole under his nose.

He was so utterly struck dumb at the sight of it that he could only stammer out:

"What—what is it? How should I know? I have done nothing, I will swear. I don't know what is the matter with the umbrella."

"You have been playing tricks with it at the office; you have been playing the fool and opening it, to show it off!" she screamed.

"I only opened it once to let them see what a nice one it was; that is all, I declare."

But she shook with rage and got up one of those conjugal scenes which make a peaceable man dread the domestic hearth more than a battlefield where bullets are raining.

She mended it with a piece of silk cut out of the old umbrella, which was of a different color, and the next day Oreille went off very humbly with the mended article in this hand. He put it into a cupboard and thought no more of it than of some unpleasant recollection.

But he had scarcely got home that evening when his wife took the umbrella from him, opened it and nearly had a fit when she saw what had befallen it, for the disaster was now irreparable. It was covered with small holes which, evidently, proceeded from burns, just as if someone had emptied the ashes from a lighted pipe onto it. It was done for utterly, irreparably.

She looked at it without a word, in too great a passion to be able to say anything. He also, when he saw the damage, remained almost dumb, in a state of frightened consternation.

They looked at each other; then he looked onto the floor. The next morment she threw the useless article at his head, screaming out in a transport of the most violent rage, for she had now recovered her voice:

"Oh, you brute! You brute! You did it on purpose, but I will pay you out for it. You shall not have another."

And then the scene began again. After the storm had raged for an hour he at last was enabled to explain himself. He declared that he could not understand it at all and that it could only proceed from malice or from vengeance.

A ring at the bell saved him; it was a friend whom they were expecting to dinner.

Mme Oreille submitted the case to him. As for buying a new umbrella, that was out of the question; her husband should not have another. The friend very sensibly said that in that case his clothes would be spoiled, and they were certainly worth more than the umbrella. But the little woman, who was still in a rage, replied:

"Very well then, when it rains he may have the kitchen umbrella, for I will not give him a new silk one."

Oreille utterly rebelled at such an idea.

"All right" he said; "then I shall resign my post. I am not going to the office with the kitchen umbrella."

The friend interposed:

"Have this one recovered; it will not cost much."

But Mme Oreille, being in the temper that she was, said:

"It will cost at least eight francs to recover it. Eight and eighteen are twenty-six. Just fancy, twenty-six francs for an umbrella! It is utter madness!"

The friend, who was only a poor man of the middle classes, had an inspiration:

"Make your fire insurance pay for it. The companies pay for all articles that are burned, as long as the damage has been done in your own house."

On hearing this advice the little woman calmed down immediately, and then after a moment's reflection she said to her husband:

"Tomorrow, before going to your office, you will go to the Maternelle Insurance Company, show them the state your umbrella is in and make them pay for the damage."

M. Oreille fairly jumped, he was so startled at the proposal.

"I would not do it for my life! It is eighteen francs lost; that is all. It will not ruin us."

The next morning he took a walking stick when he went out, for luckily it was a fine day.

Left at home alone, Mme Oreille could not get over the loss of her eighteen francs by any means. She had put the umbrella on the dining-room table, and she looked at it without being able to come to any determination.

Every moment she thought of the insuance company, but she did not dare to encounter the quizzical looks of the gentlemen who might receive her, for she was very timid before people and grew red at a mere nothing, feeling embarrassed when she had to speak to strangers.

But regret at the loss of the eighteen francs pained her as if she had been wounded. She tried not to think of it any more, and yet every moment the recollection of the loss struck her painfully. What was she to do, however?

Time went on, and she could not decide; but suddenly, like all cowards, she made up her mind.

"I will go, and we will see what will happen."

But first of all she was obliged to prepare the umbrella so that the disaster might be complete and the reason of it quite evident. She took a match from the mantelpiece, and between the ribs she burned a hole as big as the palm of her hand. Then she rolled it up carefully, fastened it with the elastic band, put on her bonnet and shawl and went quickly toward the Rue de Rivoli, where the insurance office was.

But the nearer she got the slower she walked. What was she going to say, and what reply would she get?

She looked at the numbers of the houses; there were still twenty-eight. That was all right; she had time to consider, and she walked slower and slower. Suddenly she saw a door on which was a large brass plate with "La Maternelle Insurance Office" engraved on it. Already! She waited for a moment, for she felt nervous and almost ashamed; then she went past, came back, went past again and came back again.

At last she said to herself:

"I must go in, however, so I may as well do it now as later."

She could not help noticing, however, how her heart beat as she entered. She went into an enormous room with gated wicket openings all round and a man behind each of them, and as a gentleman carrying a number of papers passed her, she stopped him and said timidly:

"I beg your pardon, monsieur, but can you tell me where I must apply for payment for anything that has been accidentally burned?"

He replied in a sonorous voice:

"The first door on the left; that is the department you want."

This frightened her still more, and she felt inclined to run away, to make no claim, to sacrifice her eighteen francs. But the idea of that sum revived her courage, and she went upstairs, out of breath, stopping at almost every other step.

She knocked at a door which she saw on the first landing, and a clear voice said in answer:

"Come in!"

She obeyed mechanically and found herself in a large room where three solemn gentlemen, each with a decoration in his buttonhole, were standing talking.

One of them asked her: "What do you want, madame?"

She could hardly get out her words but sammered: "I have come—I have come on account of an accident, something—"

He very politely pointed out a seat to her.

"If you will kindly sit down I will attend to you in a moment."

And, returning to the other two, he went on with the conversation.

"The company, gentlemen, does not consider that it is under any obligation to you for more than four hundred thousand francs, and we can pay no attention to your claim to the further sum of a hundred thousand, which you wish to make us pay. Besides that, the surveyor's valuation—"

One of the others interrupted him:

"That is quite enough, monsieur; the law courts will decide between us, and we have nothing further to do than to take our leave." And they went out after mutual ceremonious bows.

Oh, if she could only have gone away with them, how

gladly she would have done it; she would have run away and given up everything. But it was too late, for the gentleman came back and said, bowing:

"What can I do for you, madame?"

She could scarcely speak, but at last she managed to say:

"I have come—for this."

The manager looked at the object which she held out to him in mute astonishment. With trembling fingers she tried to undo the elastic and succeeded, after several attempts, and hastily opened the damaged remains of the umbrella.

"It looks to me to be in a very bad state of health," he said compassionately.

"It cost me twenty francs," she said with some hesitation.

He seemed astonished. "Really! As much as that?"

"Yes, it was a capital article, and I wanted you to see the state it is in."

"Very well, I see; very well. But I really do not understand what it can have to do with me."

She began to feel uncomfortable; perhaps this company did not pay for such small articles, and she said:

"But—it is burned."

He could not deny it.

"I see that very well," he replied.

She remained openmouthed, not knowing what to say next; then suddenly forgetting that she had left out the main thing, she said hastily:

"I am Madame Oreille; we are assured in La Maternelle, and I have come to claim the value of this damage. I only wanted you to have it recovered," she added quickly, fearing a positive refusal.

The manager was rather embarrassed and said:

"But really, madame, we do not sell umbrellas; we cannot undertake such kinds of repairs."

The little woman felt her courage reviving; she was not going to give up without a struggle; she was not even afraid now, so she said:

"I only want you to pay me the cost of repairing it; I can quite well get it done myself."

The gentleman seemed rather confused.

"Really, madame, it is such a very small matter! We are never asked to give compensation for such trivial losses. You must allow that we cannot make good pocket handkerchiefs, gloves, brooms, slippers, all the small articles which are everyday exposed to the chances of being burned." She got red and felt inclined to fly into a rage.

"But, monsieur, last December one of our chimneys caught fire and caused at least five hundred francs' damage. Monsieur Oreille made no claim on the company, and so it is only just that it should pay for my umbrella now."

The manager, guessing that she was telling a lie, said with a smile:

"You must acknowledge, madame, that it is very surprising that Monsieur Oreille should have asked no compensation for damages amounting to five hundred francs and should now claim five or six francs for mending an umbrella."

She was not the least put out and replied:

"I beg your pardon, monsieur, the five hundred francs affected Monsieur Oreille's pocket, whereas this damage, amounting to eighteen francs, concerns Madame Oreille's pocket only, which is a totally different matter."

As he saw that he had no chance of getting rid of her and that he would only be wasting his time, he said resignedly:

"Will you kindly tell me how the damage was done?"

She felt that she had won the victory and said:

"This is how it happened, monsieur: In our hall there is a bronze stick-and-umbrella stand, and the other day when I came in, I put my umbrella into it. I must tell you that just above there is a shelf for the candlesticks and matches. I put out my hand, took three or four matches and struck one, but it missed fire, so I struck another, which ignited but went out immediately, and a third did the same."

The manager interrupted her to make a joke:

"I suppose they were government matches then?"

She did not understand him and went on:

"Very likely. At any rate, the fourth caught fire, and I lit my candle and went into my room to go to bed, but in a quarter of an hour I fancied that I smelled something burning, and I have always been terribly afraid of fire. If ever we have an accident it will not be my fault, I assure you. I am terribly nervous since our chimney was on fire, as I told you, so I got up and hunted about everywhere, sniffing like a dog after game, and at last I noticed that my umbrella was buring. Most likely a match had fallen between the folds and burned it. You can see how it has damaged it."

The manager had taken his cue and asked her:

"What do you estimate the damage at?"

She did not know what to say, as she was not certain what amount to put on it, but at last she replied:

"Perhaps you had better get it done yourself. I will leave it to you."

He, however, naturally refused.

"No, madame, I cannot do that. Tell me the amount of your claim; that is all I want to know."

"Well–I think that—Look here, monsieur, I do not want to make any money out of you, so I will tell you what we will do. I will take my umbrella to the maker, who will recover it in good, durable silk, and I will bring the bill to you. Will that suit you, monsieur?"

"Perfectly, madame; we will settle it on that basis, Here is a note for the cashier, who will repay you whatever it costs you."

He gave Mme Oreille a slip of paper. She took it, got up and went out, thanking him, for she was in a hurry to escape lest he should change his mind.

She went briskly through the streets, looking out for a really good umbrella maker, and when she found a shop which appeared to be a first-class one she went in and said confidently:

"I want this umbrella recovered in silk, good silk. Use the very best and strongest you have; I don't mind what it costs."

AN ARTIFICE

THE OLD DOCTOR and his young patient were talking by the side of the fire. There was nothing really the matter with her, except that she had one of those little feminine ailments from which pretty women frequently suffer—slight anemia, nervous attack and a suspicion of fatigue, probably of that fatigue from which newly married people often suffer at the end of the first month of their married life, when they have made a love match.

She was lying on the couch and talking. "No, Doctor," she said; "I shall never be able to understand a woman deceiving her husband. Even allowing that she does not love him, that she pays no heed to her vows and promises, how can she give herself to another man? How can she conceal the intrigue from other people's eyes? How can it be possible to love amid lies and treason?"

The doctor smiled and replied: "It is perfectly easy, and I can assure you that a woman does not think of all those little subtle details when she has made up her mind to go astray. I even feel certain that no woman is ripe for true love until she has passed through all the promiscuousness and all the irksomeness of married life, which, according to an illustrious man, is nothing but an exchange of ill-tempered words by day and perfunctory caresses at night. Nothing is more true, for no woman can love passionately until after she has married.

"As for dissimulation, all women have plenty of it on hand on such occasions. The simplest of them are wonderful tacticians and extricate themselves from the greatest dilemmas in an extraordinary way."

The young woman, however, seemed incredulous. "No, Doctor," she said; "one never thinks until after it has happened of what one ought to have done in a dangerous affair, and women are certainly more liable than men to lose their heads on such occasions."

The doctor raised his hands. "After it has happened, you say! Now I will tell you something that happened to one of my female patients whom I always considered an immaculate woman.

"It happened in a provincial town. One night when I was sleeping profoundly, in that deep, first sleep from which it is so difficult to rouse yourself, it seemed to me in my dreams as if the bells in the town were sounding a fire alarm, and I woke up with a start. It was my own bell which was ringing wildly, and as my footman did not seem to be answering the door, I in turn pulled the bell at the head of my bed. Soon I heard banging and steps in the silent house, and then Jean came into my room and handed me a letter which said: 'Madame Lelièvre begs Doctor Siméon to come to her immediately.'

"I thought for a few moments, and then I said to myself: 'A nervous attack, vapors, nonsense; I am too tired.' And so I replied: 'As Doctor Siméon is not at all well, he must beg Madame Lelièvre to be kind enough to call in his colleague, Monsieur Bonnet.'

"I put the note into an envelope and went to sleep again, but about half an hour later the street bell rang again, and Jean came to me and said: 'There is somebody downstairs— I do not quite know whether it is a man or a woman, as the individual is so wrapped up—who wishes to speak to you immediately. He says it is a matter of life and death for two people.' Whereupon I sat up in bed and told him to show the person in.

"A kind of black phantom appeared who raised her veil as soon as Jean had left the room. It was Madame Bertha Lelièvre, quite a young woman, who had been married for three years to a large shopkeeper in the town and was said to have been the prettiest girl in the neighborhood.

"She was terribly pale; her face was contracted like the faces of mad people are occasionally, and her hands trembled violently. Twice she tried to speak without being able to utter a sound, but at last she stammered out:

"'Come—quick—quick, Doctor. Come—my—my lover has just died in my bedroom.' She stopped, half suffocated with emotion, and then went on: 'My husband will—be coming home from the club very soon.'

"I jumped out of bed without even considering that I was only in my night-shirt and dressed myself in a few moments. Then I said: 'Did you come a short time ago?'

"'No,' she said, standing like a statue petrified with horror. 'It was my servant—she knows.' And then after a short silence she went on: 'I was there—by his side.' And she uttered a sort of cry of horror, and after a fit of choking, which made her gasp, she wept violently, shaking with spasmodic sobs for a minute or two. Then her tears suddenly ceased, as if dried by an internal fire, and with an air of tragic calmness she said: 'Let us make haste.'

"I was ready, but I exclaimed: 'I quite forgot to order my carriage.'

"'I have one,' she said; 'it is his, which was waiting for him!' She wrapped herself up so as to completely conceal her face, and we started.

"When she was by my side in the darkness of the

carriage she suddenly seized my hand and, crushing it in her delicate fingers, she said with a shaking voice that proceeded from a distracted heart: 'Oh! If you only knew, if you only knew what I am suffering! I loved him; I have loved him distractedly, like a madwoman, for the last six months.'

"'Is anyone up in your house?' I asked.

"'No, nobody except Rose, who knows everything.'

"We stopped at the door. Evidently everybody was asleep, and we went in without making any noise by means of her latchkey and walked upstairs on tiptoe. The frightened servant was sitting on the top of the stairs with a lighted candle by her side, as she was afraid to stop by the dead man. I went into the room, which was turned upside down, as if there had been a struggle in it. The bed, which was tumbles and open, seemed to be waiting for somebody; one of the sheets was thrown onto the floor, and wet napkins with which they had bathed the young man's temples were lying by the side of a wash hand basin and a glass, while a strong smell of vinegar pervaded the room.

"The dead man's body was lying at full length in the middle of the room, and I went up to it, looked at it and touched it. I opened the eyes and felt the hands, and then, turning to the two women who were shaking as if they were frozen, I said to them: 'Help me to lift him onto the bed.' When we had laid him gently onto it I listened to his heart, put a looking glass to his lips and then said: 'It is all over; let us make haste and dress him.' It was a terrible sight!

"I took his limbs one by one, as if they had belonged to some enormous doll, and held them out to the clothes which the women brought, and they put on his socks, drawers, trousers, waistcoat and lastly the coat, but it was a difficult matter to get the arms into the sleeves.

"When it came to buttoning his boots the two women kneeled down, while I held the light. As his feet were rather swollen it was very difficult, and as they could not find a buttonhook they had to use their hairpins. When the terrible toilet was over I looked at our work and said: 'You ought to arrange his hair a little.' The girl went and brought her mistress's large-toothed comb and brush, but as she was trembling and pulling out his long, tangled hair in doing it, Mme Lelièvre took the comb out of her hand and arranged his hair as if she were caressing him. She parted it, brushed his beard, rolled his mustaches gently round her fingers, as she had no doubt been in the habit of doing in the familiarities of their intrigue.

"Suddenly, however, letting go of his hair, she took her dead lover's inert head in her hands and looked for a long time in despair at the dead face, which no longer could smile at her. Then, throwing herself onto him, she took him into her arms and kissed him ardently. Her kisses fell like blows onto his closed mouth and eyes, onto his forehead and temples, and then, putting her lips to his ear, as if he could still hear her and as if she were about to whisper something to him, to make their embraces still more ardent, she said several times in a heart-rending voice: 'Adieu, my darling!'

"Just then the clock struck twelve, and I started up. 'Twelve o'clock!' I exclaimed. 'That is the time when the club closes. Come, madame, we have not a moment to lose!'

"She started up, and I said: 'We must carry him into the drawing room.' When we had done this I placed him on a sofa and lit the chandeliers, and just then the front door was opened and shut noisily. The husband had come back, and I said: 'Rose, bring me the basin and the towels and make the room look tidy. Make haste, for heaven's sake! Monsieur Lelièvre is coming in.'

"I heard his steps on the stairs and then his hands feeling along the walls. 'Come here, my dear fellow,' I said, 'we have had an accident.'

"And the astonished husband appeared in the door with a cigar in his mouth and said: 'What is the matter? What is the meaning of this?'

"'My dear friend,' I said, going up to him, 'you find us in great embarrassment. I had remained late, chatting with your wife and our friend, who had brought me in his carriage, when he suddenly fainted, and in spite of all we have done he has remained unconscious for two hours. I did not like to call in strangers, and if you will now help me downstairs with him I shall be able to attend to him better at his own house.'

"The husband, who was surprised but quite unsuspicious, took off his hat. Then he took his rival, who would be quite inoffensive for the future, under the arms. I got between his two legs as if I had been a horse between the shafts, and we went downstairs while his wife lighted us. When we got outside I held the body up so as to deceive the coachman and said: 'Come, my friend; it is nothing; you feel better already, I expect. Pluck up your courage and make an attempt. It will soon be over.' But as I felt that he was slipping out of my hands I gave him a slap on the shoulder which sent him forward and made him fall into the carriage; then I got in after him.

"Monsieur Lelièvre, who was rather alarmed, said to me: 'Do you think it is anything serious?' To which I replied, 'No,' with a smile, as I looked at his wife, who had put her arm into that of her legitimate husband and was trying to see into the carriage.

"I shook hands with them and told my coachman to start, and during the whole drive the dead man kept falling against me. When we got to his house I said that he had become unconscious on the way home and helped to carry him upstairs, where I certified that he was dead and acted another comedy to his distracted family. At last I got back to bed, not without swearing at lovers."

The doctor ceased, though he was still smiling, and the young woman, who was in a very nervous state, said: "Why have you told me that terrible story?"

He gave her a gallant bow and replied:

"So that I may offer you my services if necessary."

HE?[1]

MY DEAR FRIEND, you cannot understand it by any possible means, you say, and I perfectly believe you. You think I am going mad? It may be so, but not for the reasons which you suppose.

Yes, I am going to get married, and I will tell you what has led me to take that step.

My ideas and my convictions have not changed at all. I look upon all legalized cohabitation as utterly stupid, for I am certain that nine husbands out of ten are cuckolds, and they get no more than their deserts for having been idiotic enough to fetter their lives and renounce their freedom in love, the only happy and good thing in the world, and for having clipped the wings of fancy which continually drive us on toward all women. You know what I mean. More than ever I feel that I am incapable of loving one woman alone, because I shall always adore all the others too much. I should like to have a thousand arms, a thousand mouths and a thousand–*temperaments*, to be able to strain an army of these charming creatures in my embrace at the same moment.

And yet I am going to get married!

I may add that I know very litle of the girl who is going to become my wife tomorrow; I have only seen her four or five times. I know that there is nothing unpleasant about

---

[1] It was in this story that the first gleams of De Maupassant's approaching madness became apparent. Thenceforward he began to revel in the strange and terrible, until his malady had seized him wholly. "The Diary of a Madman" is in a similar vein.

her, and that is enough for my purpose. She is small, fair stout, so of course the day after tomorrow I shall ardently wish for a tall, dark, thin woman.

She is not rich and belongs to the middle classes. She is a girl such as you may find by the gross, well adapted for matrimony, without any apparent faults and with no particularly striking qualities. People say of her: "Mademoiselle Lajolle is a very nice girl," and tomorrow they will say: "What a very nice woman Madame Raymon is." She belongs, in a word, to that immense number of girls who make very good wives for us till the moment comes when we discover that we happen to prefer all other women to that particular woman we married.

"Well," you will say to me, "what on earth do you get married for?"

I hardly like to tell you the strange and seemingly improbable reason that urged me on to this senseless act; the fact, however, is that I am frightened of being alone!

I don't know how to tell you or to make you understand me, but my state of mind is so wretched that you will pity and despise me.

I do not want to be alone any longer at night; I want to feel that there is someone close to me, touching me, a being who can speak and say something, no matter what it be.

I wish to be able to awaken somebody by my side, so that I may be able to ask some sudden question even, if I feel inclined, so that I may hear a human voice and feel that there is some waking soul close to me, someone whose reason is at work, so that when I hastily light the candle I may see some human face by my side—because—I am ashamed to confess it—because I am afraid of being alone.

Oh, you don't understand me yet.

I am not afraid of any danger; if a man were to come into the room I should kill him without trembling. I am not afraid of ghosts, nor do I believe in the supernatural. I am not afraid of dead people, for I believe in the total annihilation of every being that disappears from the face of this earth.

Well, yes, well, it must be told; I am afraid of myself, afraid of that horrible sensation of incomprehensible fear.

You may laugh if you like. It is terrible, and I cannot get over it. I am afraid of the walls, of the furniture, of the familiar objects, which are animated, as far as I am concerned, by a kind of animal life. Above all, I am afraid of my own dreadful thoughts, of my reason, which seems as if it were about to leave me, driven away by a mysterious and invisible agony.

At first I feel a vague uneasiness in my mind which causes a cold shiver to run all over me. I look round, and of course nothing is to be seen, and I wish there were something there, no matter what, as long as it were something tangible; I am frightened, merely because I cannot understand my own terror.

If I speak I am afraid of my own voice. If I walk I am afraid of I know not what, behind the door, behind the curtains, in the cupboard or under my bed, and yet all the time I know there is nothing anywhere, and I turn round suddenly because I am afraid of what is behind me, although there is nothing there and I know it.

I get agitated; I feel that my fear increases, and so I shut myself up in my own room, get into bed and hide under the clothes, and there, cowering down, rolled into a ball, I close my eyes in despair and remain thus for an indefinite time, remembering that my candle is alight on the table by my bedside and that I ought to put it out, and yet—I dare not do it!

It is very terrible, is it not, to be like that?

Formerly I felt nothing of all that; I came home quite comfortably and went up and down in my rooms without anything disturbing my calmness of mind. Had anyone told me that I should be attacked by a malady—for I can call it nothing else—of most improbable fear, such a stupid and terrible malady as it is, I should have laughed outright. I was certainly never afraid of opening the door in the dark; I used to go to bed slowly without locking it and never got up in the middle of the night to make sure that everything was firmly closed.

It began last year in a very strange manner, on a damp autumn evening. When my servant had left the room after I had dined I asked myself what I was going to do. I walked up and down my room for some time, feeling tired without any reason for it, unable to work and without enough energy to read. A fine rain was falling, and I felt unhappy, a prey to one of those fits of casual despondency which make us feel inclined to cry or to talk, no matter to whom, so as to shake off our depressing thoughts.

I felt that I was alone and that my rooms seemed to me to be more empty than they had ever been before. I was surrounded by a sensation of infinite and overwhelming solitude. What was I to do? I sat down, but then kind of nervous impatience agitated my legs so that I got up and began to walk about again. I was feverish, for my hands, which I had clasped behind me, as one often does when walking slowly, almost seemed to burn one another. Then suddenly a cold shiver ran down my back, and I thought the damp air might have penetrated into my room, so lit the fire for the first time that year and sat down again and looked at the flames. But soon I felt that I could not possibly remain quiet. So I got up again and determined to go out, to pull myself together and to seek a friend to bear me company.

I could not find anyone, so I went on to the boulevards to try and meet some acquaintance or other there.

I was wretched everywhere, and the wet pavement glistened in the gaslight, while the oppressive mist of the almost impalpable rain lay heavily over the streets and seemed to obscure the light from the lamps.

I went on slowly, saying to myself, "I shall not find a soul to talk to."

I glanced into several cafés, from the Madeleine as far as the Faubourg Poissonière, and saw many unhappy-looking individuals sitting at the tables, who did not seem even to have enough energy left to finish the refreshments they had ordered.

For a long time I wandered aimlessly up and down, and about midnight I started off for home; I was very calm and very tired. My concierge[2] opened the door at once, which surprised me, but I supposed that some letters had been brought up for me in the course of the evening.

I went in and found my fire still burning, so that it lighted up the room a little. In the act of taking up a candle I noticed somebody sitting in my armchair by the fire, warming his feet, with his neck toward me.

I was not in the slightest degree frightened. I thought very naturally that some friend or other had come to see me. No doubt the porter, whom I had told when I went out, had lent him his own key. In a moment I remembered all the circumstances of my return, how the street door had been opened immediately and that my own door was only latched and not locked.

---

[2] Hall porter.

I could see nothing of my friend but his head. He had evidently gone to sleep while waiting for me, so I went up to him to rouse him. I saw him quite clearly; his right arm was hanging down and his legs were crossed, while his head, which was somewhat inclined to the left of the armchair, seemed to indicate that he was asleep. "Who can it be?" I asked myself. I could not see clearly, as the room was rather dark, so I put out my hand to touch him on the shoulder, and it came in contact with the back of the chair. There was nobody there; the seat was empty.

I fairly jumped with fright. For a moment I drew back as if some terrible danger had suddenly appeared in my way; then I turned round again, impelled by some imperious desire to look at the armchair again. I remained standing upright, panting with fear, so upset that I could not collect my thoughts, and ready to drop.

But I am naturally a cool man and soon recovered myself. I thought: "It is a mere hallucination; that is all," and I immediately began to reflect about this phenomenon. Thoughts fly very quickly at such moments.

I had been suffering from a hallucination; that was an incontestable fact. My mind had been perfectly lucid and had acted regularly and logically, so there was nothing the matter with the brain. It was only my eyes that had been deceived; they had had a vision, one of those visions which lead simple folk to believe in miracles. It was a nervous accident to the optical apparatus, nothing more; the eyes were rather overwrought, perhaps.

I lit my candle, and when I stooped down to the fire in so doing I noticed that I was trembling, and I raised myself up with a jump, as if somebody had touched me from behind.

I was certainly not by any means reassured.

I walked up and down a little and hummed a tune or two. Then I double-locked my door and felt rather reassured; now, at any rate, nobody could come in.

I sat down again and thought over my adventure for a long time; then I went to bed and put out my light.

For some minutes all went well; I lay quietly on my back. Then an irresistible desire seized me to look round the room, and I turned onto my side.

My fire was nearly out, and the few glowing embers threw a faint light on to the floor by the chair, where I fancied I saw the man sitting again.

I quickly struck a match, but I had been mistaken, for there was nothing there; I got up, however, and hid the chair behind my bed and tried to get to sleep as the room was now dark. But I had not forgotten myself for more than five minutes when in my dream I saw all the scene which I had witnessed as clearly as if it were reality. I woke up with a start and, having lit the candle, sat up in bed without venturing even to try and go to sleep again.

Twice, however, sleep overcame me for a few moments in spite of myself, and twice I saw the same thing again; till I fancied I was going mad. When day broke, however, I thought that I was cured and slept peacefully till noon.

It was all past and over. I had been feverish, had had the nightmare; I don't know what. I had been ill, in a word, but yet I thought that I was a great fool.

I enjoyed myself thoroughly that evening; I went and dined at a restaurant; afterward I went to the theater and then started home. But as I got near the house I was seized by a strange feeling of uneasiness once more; I was afraid of *seeing* him again. I was not afraid of him, not afraid of his presence, in which I did not believe, but I was afraid of being deceived again; I was afraid of some fresh hallucination, afraid lest fear should take possession of me.

For more than an hour I wandered up and down the pavement; then I thought that I was really too foolish and returned home. I panted so that I could scarcely get upstairs and remained standing outside my door for more than ten minutes; then suddenly I took courage and pulled myself together. I inserted my key into the lock and went in with a candle in my hand. I kicked open my half-open bedroom door and gave a frightened look toward the fireplace; there was nothing there. Ah!.

What a relief and what a delight! What a deliverance; I walked up and down briskly and boldly, but I was not altogether reassured and kept turning round with a jump; the very shadows in the corners disquieted me.

I slept badly and was constantly disturbed by imaginary noises, but I did not see *him;* no, that was all over.

Since that time I have been afraid of being alone at night. I feel that the specter is there close to me, around me, but it has not appeared to me again. And supposing it did, what would it matter, since I do not believe in it and know that it is nothing?

It still worries me, however, because I am constantly thinking of it: *his right arm hanging down and his head inclined to the left like a man who was asleep.* Enough of that, in heaven's name! I don't want to think about it!

Why, however, am I so persistently possessed with this idea? His feet were close to the fire!

He haunts me; it is very stupid, but so it is. Who and what is HE? I know that he does not exist except in my cowardly imagination, in my fears and in my agony! There—enough of that!

Yes, it is all very well for me to reason with myself, to

stiffen myself, so to say, but I cannot remain at home because I knew he is there. I know I shall not see him again; he will not show himself again; that is all over. But he is there all the same in my thoughts. He remains invisible, but that does not prevent his being there. He is behind the doors, in the closed cupboards, in the wardrobe, under the bed, in every dark corner. If I open the door or the cupboard, if I take the candle to look under the bed and throw a light onto the dark places, he is there no longer, but I feel that he is behind me. I turn round, certain that I shall not see him, that I shall never see him again, but he is, nonetheless, behind me.

It is very stupid; it is dreadful, but what am I to do? I cannot help it.

But if there were two of us in the place I feel certain that he would not be there any longer, for he is there just because I am alone, simply and solely because I am alone!

FRANCIS

WE WERE GOING OUT of the asylum when I perceived in one corner of the courtyard a tall thin man who was forever calling an imaginary dog. He would call out with a sweet and tender voice: "Cocotte, my little Cocotte; come here, Cocotte; come here, my beauty," striking his leg, as one does to attract the attention of an animal. I asked the doctor what the matter was with the man.

"Oh, that is an interesting case," he said; "he is a coachman named Francis, and he became insane from drowning his dog."

I insisted upon his telling me the story. The most simple and humble things sometimes strike most to our hearts.

And here is the adventure of this man which was known solely to a groom, his comrade.

In the suburbs of Paris lived a rich, middle-class family. Their villa was in the midst of a park, on the bank of the Seine. Their coachman was this Francis, a country boy, a little awkward, but of good heart, simple and easily duped.

When he was returning one evening to his master's house a dog began to follow him. At first he took no notice of it, but the persistence of the beast in walking on his heels caused him finally to turn around. He looked to see if he knew this dog. No, he had never seen it before.

The dog was frightfully thin and had great hanging dugs. She totted behind the man with a woeful, famished look, her tail between her legs, her ears close to her head, and stopped when he stopped, starting again when he started.

He tried to drive away this skeleton of a beast. "Get out! If you want to save yourself—Go, now! Hou! Hou!" She would run away a few steps and then sit down, waiting; then when the coachman started on again, she followed behind him.

He made believe to pick up stones. The animal fled a little way with a great shaking of the flabby mammillae, but followed again as soon as the man turned his back.

Then the coachman Francis took pity and called her. The dog approached timidly, her back bent in a circle and all the ribs showing under the skin. The man smoothed these projecting bones and, moved by pity for the misery of the beast, said: "Come along then!" Immediately the tail began to move; she felt the welcome, the adoption, and instead of staying at her new master's heels she began to run ahead of him.

He installed her on some straw in his stable, then ran to the kitchen in search of bread. When she had eaten her fill she went to sleep, curled up, ringlike.

The next day the coachman told his master who allowed him to keep the animal. She was a good beast, intelligent and faithful, affectionate and gentle.

But immediately they discovered in her a terrible fault. She was inflamed with love from one end of the year to the other. In a short time she had made the acquaintance of every dog about the country, and they roamed about the place day and night. With the indifference of a girl, she shared her favors with them, feigning to like each one best, dragging behind her a veritable mob composed of many different models of the barking race, some as large as a fist, others as tall as an ass. She took them to walk through routes with interminable courses, and when she stopped to rest in the shade they made a circle about her and looked at her with tongues hanging out.

The people of the country considered her a phenomenon; they had never seen anything like it. The veterinary could not understand it.

When she returned to the stable in the evening the crowd of dogs made seige for proprietorship. They wormed their way through every crevice in the hedge which inclosed the park, devastated the flower beds, broke down the flowers, dug holes in the urns, exasperating the gardener. They would howl the whole night about the building where their friend lodged, and nothing could persuade them to go away.

In the daytime they even entered the house. It was an invasion, a plague, a calamity. The people of the house met at any moment on the staircase, and even in the rooms, little yellow pug dogs with tails decorated, hunting dogs, bulldogs, wolfhounds with filthy skin, vagabonds without life or home, besides some new-world enormities which frightened the children.

All the unknown dogs for ten miles around came, from one knew not where, and lived, no one knew how, disappearing all together.

Nevertheless, Francis adored Cocotte. He had named her Cocotte, "without malice, sure that she merited her name." And he repeated over and over again: "This beast is a person. It only lacks speech."

He had a magnificent collar in red leather made for her, which bore these words, engraved on a copperplate: "Mlle Cocotte, from Francis, the coachman."

She became enormous. She was as fat as she had been thin, her body puffed out, under which hung always the long, swaying mammillae. She had fattened suddenly and walked with difficulty, the paws wide apart, after the fashion of people that are too large, the mouth open for breath, wide open as soon as she tried to run.

She showed a phenomenal fecundity, producing, four times a year, a litter of litle animals, belonging to all varieties of the canine race. Francis, after having chosen the one he would leave her "to take the milk," would pick up the others in his stable apron and pitilessly throw them into the river.

Soon the cook joined her complaints to those of the gardener. She found dogs under her kitchen range, in the cupboards and in the coalbin, always fleeing whenever she encountered them.

The master, becoming impatient, ordered Francis to get rid of Cocotte. The man, inconsolable, tried to place her somewhere. No one wanted her. Then he resolved to lose her and put her in charge of a wagoner who was to leave her in the country the other side of Paris, beyond De Joinville-le-Pont.

That same evening Cocotte was back.

It became necessary to take measures. For the sum of five francs they persuaded a cook on the train to Havre to take her. He was to let her loose when they arrived.

At the end of three days she appeared again in her stable, harassed, emaciated, exhausted.

The master was merciful and insisted on nothing further.

But the dogs soon returned in greater numbers than ever and were more provoking. And as they were giving a great dinner one evening a stuffed chicken was carried off by a dog under the nose of the cook, who dared not dispute the right to it.

This time the master was angry and, calling Francis to him, said hotly: "If you don't kick this beast into the water tomorrow morning I shall put you out, do you understand?"

The man was undone, but he went up to his room to pack his trunk, preferring to leave the place. Then he reflected that he would not be likely to get in anywhere else, dragging this unwelcome beast behind him; he remembered that he was in a good house, well paid and well fed, and he said to himself that it was not worth while giving up all this for a dog. He enumerated his own interests and finished by resolving to get rid of Cocotte at dawn the next day.

However, he slept badly. At daybreak he was up and, preparing a strong cord, he went in search of the dog. She arose slowly, shook herself, stretched her limbs and came to greet her master. Then his courage failed and he began to stroke her tenderly, smoothing her long ears, kissing her on the muzzle lavishing upon her all the loving names that he knew.

A neighboring clock struck; he could no longer hesitate. He opened the door. "Come," he said. The beast wagged her tail, understanding only that she was to go out.

They reached the bank and chose a place where the water seemed deepest. Then he tied one end of the cord to the beautiful leather collar and, taking a great stone, attached it to the other end. Then he seized Cocotte in his arms and kissed her furiously, as one does when he is taking leave of a person. Then he held her right around the neck, fondling her and calling her "My pretty Cocotte, my little Cocotte," and she responded as best she could, growling with pleasure.

Ten times he tried to throw her in, and each time his heart failed him. Then abruptly he decided to do it and, with all his force, hurled her as far as possible. She tried at first to swim, as she did when taking a bath, but her head, dragged by the stone, went under again and again. She threw her master a look of despair, a human look, battling, as a person does when drowning. Then before the whole body sank, the hind paws moved swiftly in the water; then they disappeared also.

For five minutes bubbles of air came to the surface as if the river had begun to boil. And Francis, haggard, excited, with heart palpitating, believed he saw Cocotte writhing in the slime. And he said to himself with the simplicity of a peasant: "What does she think of me by this time, that beast?"

He almost became idiotic. He was sick for a month and each night saw the dog again. He felt her licking his hands; he heard her bark.

It was necessary to call a physician. Finally he grew better, and his master and mistress took him to their estate near Rouen.

There he was still on the bank of the Seine. He began to take baths. Every morning he went down with the groom to swim across the the river.

One day, as they were amusing themselves splashing in the water, Francis suddenly cried out to his companion:

"Look at what is coming toward us. I am going to make you taste a cutlet."

It was an enormous carcass, swelled and stripped of its hair, its paws moving forward in the air, following the current.

Francis approached it, making his jokes:

"What a prize, my boy! My! But it is not fresh! It is not thin; that is sure!"

And he turned about, keeping at a distance from the

great putrefying body.

Then suddenly he kept still and looked at it in stange fashion. He approached it again, this time near enough to touch. He examined carefully the collar, took hold of the leg, seized the neck, made it turn over, drew it toward him and read upon the green copper that still adhered to the discolored leather: "Mlle Cocotte, from Francis, the coachman."

The dead dog had found her master sixty miles from their home!

He uttered a fearful cry and began to swim with all his might toward the bank, shouting all the way. And when he reached the land he ran, all bare through the country. He was mad!

WAS IT A DREAM?

I HAD LOVED her madly!

Why does one love? Why does one love? How queer it is to see only one being in the world, to have only one thought in one's mind, only one desire in the heart and only one name on the lips—a name which comes up continually, rising, like the water in a spring, from the depths of the soul to the lips, a name which one repeats over and over again, which one whispers ceaselessly, everywhere, like a prayer.

I am going to tell you our story, for love only has one, which is always the same. I met her and lived on her tenderness, on her caresses, in her arms, in her dresses, on her words, so completely wrapped up, bound and absorbed in everything which came from her that I no longer cared whether it was day or night, or whether I was dead or alive, on this old earth of ours.

And then she died. How? I do not know; I no longer know anything. But one evening she came home wet, for it was raining heavily, and the next day she coughed, and she coughed for about a week and took to her bed. What happened I do not remember now, but doctors came, wrote and went away. Medicines were brought, and some women made her drink them. Her hands were hot, her forehead was burning, and her eyes bright and sad. When I spoke to her she answered me, but I do not remember what we said. I have forgotten everything, everything, everything! She died, and I very well remember her slight, feeble sigh.

The nurse said: "Ah!" and I understood; I understood!

I knew nothing more, nothing. I saw a priest who said: "Your mistress?" And it seemed to me as if he were insulting her. As she was dead, nobody had the right to say that any longer, and I turned him out. Another came who was very kind and tender, and I shed tears when he spoke to me about her.

They consulted me about the funeral, but I do not remember anything that they said, though I recollected the coffin and the sound of the hammer when they nailed her down in it. Oh! God, God!

She was buried! Buried! She! In that hole! Some people came—female friends. I made my escape and ran away. I ran and then walked through the streets, went home and the next day started on a journey.

. . . .

Yesterday I returned to Paris, and when I saw my room again—our room, our bed, our furniture, everything that remains of the life of a human being after death—I was seized by such a violent attack of fresh grief that I felt like opening the window and throwing myself out into the street. I could not remain any longer among these things, between these walls which had inclosed and sheltered her, which retained a thousand atoms of her, of her skin and of her breath, in their imperceptible crevices. I took up my hat to make my escape, and just as I reached the door I passed the large glass in the hall, which she had put there so that she might look at herself every day from head to foot as she went out, to see if her toilet looked well and was correct and pretty from her little boots to her bonnet.

I stopped short in front of that looking glass in which she had so often been reflected—so often, so often, that it must have retained her reflection. I was standing there trembling with my eyes fixed on the glass—on that flat, profound, empty glass—which had contained her entirely and had possessed her as much as I, as my passionate looks had. I felt as if I loved the glass. I touched it; it was cold. Oh, the recollection! Sorrowful mirror, burning mirror, horrible mirror, to make men suffer such torments! Happy is the man whose heart forgets everything that it has contained, everything that has passed before it, everything that has looked at itself in it or has been reflected in its affection, in its love! How I suffer!

I went out without knowing it, without wishing it, and toward the cemetery. I found her simple grave, a white marble cross, with these few words:

She loved, was loved and died.

She is there below, decayed! How horrible! I sobbed with my forehead on the ground, and I stopped there for a long time, a long time. Then I saw that it was getting dark and a strange, mad wish, the wish of a despairing lover, seized me. I wished to pass the night, the last night, in weeping on her grave. But I should be seen and driven out. How was I to manage? I was cunning and got up and began to roam about in that city of the dead. I walked and walked. How small this city is in comparison with the other, the city in which we live. And yet how much more numerous the dead are than the living. We want high houses, wide streets and much room for the four generations who see the daylight at the same time, drink water from the spring and wine from the vines and eat bread from the plains.

And for all the generations of the dead, for all that ladder of humanity that has descended down to us, there is scarcely anything, scarcely anything! The earth takes them back, and oblivion effaces them. Adieu!

At the end of the cemetery I suddenly perceived that I was in its oldest part, where those who had been dead a long time are mingling with the soil, where the crosses themselves are decayed, where possibly newcomers will be put tomorrow. It is full of untended roses, of strong and dark cypress trees, a sad and beautiful garden, nourished on human flesh.

I was alone, perfectly alone. So I crouched in a green tree and hid myself there completely amid the thick and somber branches. I waited, clinging to the stem like a shipwrecked man does to a plank.

When it was quite dark I left my refuge and began to walk softly, slowly, inaudibly, through that ground full of dead people. I wandered about for a long time but could not find her tomb again. I went on with extended arms, knocking against the tombs with my hands, my feet, my knees, my chest, even with my head, without being able to find her. I groped about like a blind man finding his way; I felt the stones, the crosses, the iron railings, the metal wreaths and the wreaths of faded flowers! I read the names with my fingers, by passing them over the letters. What a night! What a night! I could not find her again!

There was no moon. What a night! I was frightened, horribly frightened in these narrow paths between two rows of graves. Graves! Graves! Graves! Nothing but graves! On my right, on my left, in front of me, everywhere there were graves! I sat down on one of them, for I could not walk any longer; my knees were so weak. I could hear my heart beat! And I heard something else as well. What? A confused, nameless noise. Was the noise in my head, in the impenetrable night or beneath the mysterious earth, the earth sown with human corpses? I looked all around me, but I cannot say how long I remained there; I was paralyzed with terror, cold with fright, ready to shout out, ready to die.

Suddenly it seemed to me that the slab of marble on which I was sitting was moving. Certainly it was moving, as if it were being raised. With a bound I sprang onto the neighboring tomb, and I saw, yes, I distinctly saw the stone which I had just quitted rise upright. Then the dead person appeared, a naked skeleton, pushing the stone back with its bent back. I saw it quite clearly, although the night was so dark. On the cross I could read:

Here lies Jacques Olivant, who died at the age of fifty-one. He loved his family, was kind and honorable and died in the grace of the Lord.

The dead man also read what was inscribed on the tombstone; then he picked up a stone off the path, a little, pointed stone, and began to scrape the letters carefully. He slowly effaced them, and with the hollows of his eyes he looked at the places where they had been engraved. Then with the tip of the bone that had been his forefinger he wrote in luminous letters, like those lines which boys trace on walls with the tip of a lucifer match:

Here reposes Jacques Olivant, who died at the age of fifty-one. He hastened his father's death by his unkindness, as he wished to inherit his fortune; he tortured his wife, tormented his children, deceived his neighbors, robbed everyone he could and died wretched.

When he had finished writing, the dead man stood motionless, looking at his work. On turning around I saw that all the graves were open, that all the dead bodies had emerged from them and that all had effaced the lines inscribed on the gravestones by their relations substituting the truth instead. And I saw that all had been the tormentors of their neighbors—malicious, dishonest, hypocrites, liars, rogues, calumniators, envious; that they had stolen, deceived, performed every disgraceful, every abominable action, these good fathers, these faithful wives, these devoted sons, these chaste daughters, these honest tradesmen, these men and women who were called irreproachable. They were all writing at the same time, on the threshold of their eternal abode, the truth, the terrible and the holy truth of which everybody was ignorant, or pretended to be ignorant, while they were alive.

I thought that *she* also must have written something on her tombstone and now, running without any fear among the half-open coffins, among the corpses and skeletons, I went toward her, sure that I should find her immediately. I recognized her at once without seeing her face, which was covered by the winding sheet, and on the marble cross where shortly before I had read:

She loved, was loved and died.

I now saw:

Having gone out in the rain one day in order to deceive her lover, she caught cold and died.

. . . .

It appears that they found me at daybreak, lying on the grave, unconscious.

THE DEAF-MUTE

My dear friend, you ask me why I do not return to Paris; you will be astonished and almost angry, I suppose, when I give you the reason, which will, without doubt, be revolting to you: "Why should a hunter return to Paris at the height of the woodcock season?"

Certainly I understand and like life in the city very well, that life which leads from the chamber to the sidewalk, but I prefer a freer life, the rude life of the hunter in autumn.

In Paris it seems to me that I am never out of doors; for, in fact, the streets are only great, common apartments without a ceiling. Is one in the air between two walls, his feet upon stone or wooden pavement, his view shut in everywhere by buildings, without any horizon of verdure, fields or wood? Thousands of neighbors jostle you, push you, salute you and talk with you, but the fact of receiving water upon an umbrella when it rains is not sufficient to give me the impression or the sensation of space.

Here I perceive clearly and deliciously the difference between indoors and out. But it was not of that that I wish to speak to you.

Well then, the woodcocks are flying.

And it is necessary to tell you that I live in a great Norman house, in a valley, near a little river, and that I hunt nearly every day.

Other days I read; I even read things that men in Paris have not the time to become acquainted with, very serious things, very profound, very curious, written by a brave, scholarly genius, a foreigner who had spent his life studying the subject and observing the facts relative to the influence of the functions of our organs upon our intelligence.

But I was speaking to you of woodcocks.

My two friends, the D'Orgemol brothers, and myself remain here during the hunting season, awaiting the first frost. Then when it freezes we set out for their farm in Cannetot, near Fécamp, because there is a delicious little wood there, a divine wood, where every woodcock that flies comes to lodge.

You know the D'Orgemols, those two giants, those Normans of ancient times, those two males of the old, powerful conquering race which invaded France, took England and kept it, established itself on every coast of the world, made towns everywhere, passed like a flood over Sicily, creating there popes in their priestly tricks and ridiculed them, more sly than the Italian pontiffs themselves, and above all, left children in all the beds of the world. These D'Orgemols are two Normans of the best stamp and are all Norman—voice, accent, mind, blond hair and eyes, which are the color of the sea.

When we are together we talk the patois; we live, think and act in Norman; we become Norman landowners, more peasants than farmers.

For two weeks now we have been waiting for woodcocks. Every morning Simon, the elder, will say: "Hey! Here's the wind coming round to the east, and it's going to freeze. In two days they will be here."

The younger, Gaspard, more exact, waits for the frost to come before he announces it.

But last Thursday he entered my room at dawn, crying out:

"It has come! The earth is all white. Two days more and we shall go to Cannetot."

Two days later, in fact, we do set out for Cannetot. Certainly you would have laughed to see us. We take our places in a strange sort of hunting wagon that my father had constructed long ago. Constructed is the only word that I can use in speaking of this monstrous carriage, or rather this earthquake on wheels. There was room for everything inside: a place for provisions, a place for the guns, place for the trunks and places of clear space for the dogs. Everything is sheltered except the men, perched on seats as high as a third story, and all this supported by four gigantic wheels. One mounted as best he could, making his feet, hands and even his teeth serve him for the occasion, for there was no step to give access to the edifice.

Now the two D'Orgemols and myself scaled this mountain, clothed like Laplanders. We have on sheepskins, wear enormous, woolen stockings outside our pantaloons and gaiters outside our woolen stockings; we also have some black fur caps and white fur gloves. When we are installed, John, my servant, throws us our three terriers, Pif, Faf and Mustache. Pif belongs to Simon, Paf to Gaspard and Mustache to me. They look like three crocodiles covered with hair. They are long, low, and crooked, with bent legs and so hairy that they have the look of a yellow thicket. Their eyes can scarcely be seen under their eyebrows, or their teeth through their beards. One could never shut them into the rolling kennels of the carriage. Each one puts his own dog under his feet to keep him warm.

And now we are off, shivering abominably. It is cold

and freezing hard. We are contented. Toward five o'clock we arrive. The farmer, Master Picot, is expecting us, waiting before the door. He is also a jolly fellow, not tall, but round, squat, vigorous as a bulldog, sly as a fox, always laughing, always contented, knowing how to make money out of all of us.

It is a great festival for him when the woodcock arrives. The farm is large, and on it an old building set in an apple orchard, surrounded by four rows of beech trees, which battle against the winds from the sea all the year.

We enter the kitchen where a bright fire is burning in our honor. Our table is set against the high chimney, where a large chicken is turning and roasting before the clear flame, and whose gravy is running into an earthen dish beneath.

The farmer's wife salutes us, a tall, quiet woman, wholly occupied with the cares of her house, her head full of accounts, the price of grain, of poultry, of mutton and beef. She is an orderly woman, set and severe, known for her worth in the neighborhood.

At the end of the kitchen is set the long table where all the farm hands, drivers, laborers, stableboys, shepherds and woman servants sit down. They eat in silence under the active eye of the mistress, watching us dine with Master Picot, who says witty things to make us laugh. Then, when all her servants are fed, Mme Picot takes her repast alone at one corner of the table, a rapid and frugal repast, watching the serving maid meanwhile. On ordinary days she dines with all the rest.

We all three sleep, the D'Orgemols and myself, in a bare, white room, whitewashed with lime, containing only our three beds, three chairs and three basins.

Gaspard always wakes first and sounds the echoing watchword. In half an hour everybody is ready, and we set out with Master Picot who hunts with us.

M. Picot prefers me to his masters. Why? Without doubt because I am not his master. So we two reach the woods by the right, while the two brothers come to the attack by the left. Simon has the care of the dogs, all three attached to the end of a rope.

For we are not hunting woodcock but the wolf. We are convinced that it is better to find the woodcock than to seek it. If one falls upon one and kills it, there you are! But when one specially wishes to meet one, he can never quite bring him down. It is truly a beautiful and curious thing, hearing the loud report of a gun in the fresh morning air and then the formidable voice of Gaspard filling the space as he howls:

"Woodcock! There it is."

As for me, I am sly. When I have killed a woodcock I cry out: "Wolf!" And then I triumph in my success when we go to a clear place for the midday lunch.

Here we are then, Master Picot and I, in the little woods, where the leaves fall with a sweet and continued murmur, with a dry murmur, a little sad, for they are dead. It is cold, a light cold which stings the eyes, the nose and the ears and powders with a fine, white moss the limbs of the trees and the brown, plowed earth. But there is warmth through all our limbs under the great sheepskin. The sun is gay in the blue air which it warms scarcely at all, but it is gay. It is good to hunt in the woods on fresh mornings in winter.

Down below a dog is loudly baying. It is Pif. I know his thin voice but it ceases. Then there is another, and Paf in his turn begins to bark. And what has become of Mustache? Ah, there is a little cry like that of a chicken being strangled! They have stirred up a wolf. Attention,

Master Picot!

They separate, then approach each other, scatter again and then return; we follow their unforeseen windings, coming out into little roads, the mind on the alert, finger on the trigger of the gun.

They turn toward the fields again, and we turn also. Suddenly there is a gray spot, a shadow, crossing the bypath. I aim and fire. The light smoke rises in the blue air, and I perceive under a bush a bit of white hair which moves. Then I shout with all my force, "Wolf, wolf! There he is!" And I show him to the three dogs, the three hairy crocodiles, who thank me by wagging their tails. Then they go off in search of another.

Master Picot joins me. Mustache begins to yap. The farmer says: "There must be a hare there at the edge of the field."

The moment that I came out of the wood I perceived, not ten steps from me, enveloped in his immense, yellowish mantle and wearing his knitted, woolen cap such as shepherds wear at home, Master Picot's herdsman Gargan, the deaf-mute. I said, "Good morning," to him, according to our custom, and he raised his hand to salute me. He had not heard my voice, but had seen the motion of my lips.

For fifteen years I had known this shepherd. For fifteen years I had seen him each autumn on the border or in the middle of the field, his body motionless and always knitting in his hands. His flock followed him like a pack of hounds, seeming to obey his eye.

Master Picot now took me by the arm, saying:

"Did you know that the shepherd killed his wife?"

I was stupefied. "What, Gargan—the deaf-mute?"

"Yes, this winter, and his case was tried at Rouen. I

will tell you about it."

And he led me into the underbrush, for the shepherd knew how to catch words from his master's lips, as if he heard them spoken. He could understand only him; but, watching his face closely, he was no longer deaf, and the master, on the other hand, seemed to divine, like a sorcerer, the meaning of all the mute's pantomime, the gestures of his fingers, the expression of his face and the motion of his eyes.

Here is his simple story, the various, somber facts as they came to pass:

Gargan was the son of a marl digger, one of those men who go down into the marlp it to extract that kind of soft, dissolving stone, sown under the soil. A deaf-mute by birth, he had been brought up to watch the cows along the ditches by the side of the roads.

Then, picked up by Picot's father, he had become the shepherd on his farm. He was an excellent shepherd, devout, upright, knowing how to find the lost members of his flock, although nobody had taught him anything.

When Picot took the farm in his turn, Gargan was thirty years old and looked forty. He was tall, thin and bearded— bearded like a patriarch.

About this time a good woman of the country, Mme Martel, died very poor, leaving a girl fifteen years old who was called "Drops," because of her immoderate love for brandy.

Picot took in this ragged waif, employed her in light duties, giving her a home without pay in return for her work. She slept under the barn, in the stable or the cow house, upon straw or on the manure heap, anywhere, it mattered not where, for they could not give a bed to this barefoot. She slept, then, no matter where, with no matter whom, perhaps with the plowman or the stableboy. But it happened soon that she gave her attention to the deaf-mute and coupled herself with him in a continued fashion. What united these two miserable beings? How had they understood each other? Had he ever known a woman before this barn rover, he who had never talked with anyone? Was it she who found him in his wheeled hut and seduced him, like an Eve of the rut, at the edge of the road? No one knows. They only know that one day they were living together as husband and wife.

No one was astonished by it, and Picot found it a very natural coupling. But the curate heard of this union without a Mass and was angry. He reproached Mme Picot, disturbed her conscience and threatened her with mysterious punishments. What was to be done? It was very simple. They must go and be married at the church and at the mayor's. They had nothing, either of them: he, not a whole pair of pantaloons, she, not a petticoat of a single kind of cloth. So there was nothing to oppose what the law and religion required. They were united in an hour before the mayor and the curate and believed that all was regulated for the best.

Now it soon became a joke in the country (pardon the villainous word) to make a deceived husband of this poor Gargan. Before she was married, no one thought of sleeping with "Drops," but now each one wished his turn, for the sake of a laughable story. Everybody went there for a little glass behind the husband's back. The affair made so much noise that even some of the Goderville gentlemen came to see her.

For a half pint "Drops" would finish the spectacle with no matter whom, in a ditch, behind a wall, anywhere, while the silhouette of the motionless Gargan could be seen knitting a stocking not a hundred feet from there, surrounded by his bleating flock. And they laughed about it enough to make themselves ill in all the cafés of the country. If was the only thing talked of in the evening before the fire, and upon the road the first thing one would ask: "Have you paid your drop to 'Drops'?" Everyone knew what that meant.

The shepherd never seemed to see anything. But one day the Poirot boy, of Sasseville, called to Gargan's wife from behind the mill, showing her a full bottle. She understod and ran to him, laughing. Now scarcely were they engaged in their criminal deed when the herdsman fell upon them as if he had come out of a cloud. Poirot fled at full speed, his breeches about his heels, while the deaf-mute, with a cry of a beast, sprang at his wife's throat.

The people working in the fields ran toward them. It was too late; her tongue was black; her eyes were coming out of her head; the blood was flowing from her nose. She was dead.

The shepherd was tried by the judge at Rouen. As he was a mute, Picot served as interpreter. The details of the affair amused the audience very much. But the farmer had but one idea: his herdsman must be acquitted. And he went about it in earnest.

At first he related the deaf-mute's whole story, including that of his marriage; then when he came to the crime, he himself questioned the assassin.

The assemblage was very quiet.

Picot pronounced the words slowly: "Did you know that she had deceived you?" And at the same time he asked the question with his eyes in pantomime.

The other answered "No" with his head.

"Were you asleep in the mill when you surprised her?"

And he made a gesture of a man seeing some disgusting thing.

The other answered "Yes" with his head.

Then the farmer, imitating the signs of the mayor who married them and of the priest who united them in the name of God, asked his servant if he had killed his wife because she was bound to him before men and before heaven.

The shepherd answered "Yes" with his head.

Picot then said to him: "Come, tell us how it happened."

Then the deaf-mute reproduced the whole scene in pantomime. He showed how he was asleep in the mill, that he was awakened by feeling the straw move, that he had watched quietly and had seen the whole thing.

He rose between the two policemen and brusquely imitated the obscene movement of the criminal couple entangled before him.

A tumultuous laugh went through the hall then stopped short, for the herdsman, with haggard eyes, moving his jaw and his great beard as if he had bitten something, with arms extended and head thrown forward, repeated the terrible action of a murderer who strangles a being.

And he howled frightfully, so excited with anger that one would think he believed he still held her in his grasp, and the policemen were obliged to seize him and seat him by force in order to calm him.

A great shiver of agony ran through the assembly. Then Master Picot, placing his hand upon his servant's shoulder, said simply: "He knows what honor is, this man does."

And the shepherd was acquitted.

As for me, my dear friend, I listened to this adventure to its close, much moved, and have related it to you in gross terms in order not to change the farmer's story. But now there is a report of a gun from the woods, and the formidable voice of Gaspard is heard growling in the wind, like the sound of a cannon:

"Woodcock! There is one."

And this is how I employ my time, watching for the woodcock to pass, while you are also going to the Bois to see the first winter costumes.

SENTIMENT

IT WAS during the hunting season at the country seat of the De Bannevilles. The autumn was rainy and dull. The red leaves, instead of crackling under foot, rotted in the hollows after the heavy showers.

The forest, almost leafless, was as humid as a bathroom. There was a moldy odor under the great trees, stripped of their fruits, which enveloped one on entering, as if a lye had been made from the steeped herbs, the soaked earth and the continuous rainfall. The hunters' ardor was dampened; the dogs were sullen, their tails lowered and their hair matted against their sides, while the young huntresses, their habits drenched with rain, returned each evening, depressed in body and spirit.

In the great drawing room after dinner they played lotto, but without enthusiasm, as the wind made a clattering noise upon the shutters and forced the old weather vanes into a spinning-top tournament. Someone suggested telling stories as they are told in books, but no one could think of anything very amusing. The hunters narrated some of their adventures with the gun, the slaughter of wolves, for example, and the ladies racked their brains without finding anywhere the imagination of Scheherazade.

They were about to abandon this form of diversion, when a young lady, carelessly playing with the hand of her old, unmarried aunt, noticed a little ring made of blond hair, which she had often seen before but thought nothing about.

Moving it gently about the finger, she said suddenly: "Tell us the history of this ring, Auntie; it looks like the hair of a child—"

The old maiden reddened and then grew pale, then in a trembling voice she replied: "It is sad, so sad that I never care to speak about it. All the unhappiness of my life is centered in it. I was young then, but the memory of it remains so painful that I weep whenever I think of it."

They wished very much to hear the story, but the aunt refused to tell it; finally they urged so much that she at length consented.

"You have often heard me speak of the Santèze family, now extinct. I knew the last three men of this family. They all died within three months in the same manner. This hair belonged to the last one. He was thirteen years old when he killed himself for me. That appears very strange to you, doesn't it?

"It was a singular race, a race of fools, if you will, but of charming fools, of fools for love. All, from father to son, had these violent passions, waves of emotion, which drove them to deeds most exalted, to fanatical devotion and even to crime. Devotion was to them what it is to certain religious souls. Those who become monks are not of the same nature as drawing-room favorites. One might almost say, as a proverb, 'He loved like a Santèze.'

"To see them was to divine this characteristic. They all had curly hair, growing low upon the brow, beard crinkly, eyes large, very large, whose rays seemed to penetrate and disturb you, without your knowing just why.

"The grandfather of the one of whom this is the souvenir, after many adventures and some duels on account of entanglements with women, when toward sixty became passionately taken with the daughter of his farmer. I knew them both. She was blonde, pale, distinguished looking, with a soft voice and a sweet look, so sweet that she reminded one of a Madonna. The old lord took her home with him and immediately became so captivated that he was unable to pass a minute away from her. His daughter and his daughter-in-law, who lived in the house, found this perfectly natural, so much was love a tradition of the family. When one was moved by a great passion nothing surprised them, and if anyone expressed a different notion before them, of disunited lovers or revenge after some treachery, they would both say in the same desolate voice: 'Oh, how he (or she) must have suffered before coming to that!' Nothing more. They were moved with pity by all dramas of the heart and never spoke slightingly of them, even when they were unworthy.

"One autumn a young man, Monsieur de Gradelle, invited for the hunting, eloped with the young woman.

"Monsieur de Santèze remained calm, as if nothing had happened. But one morning they found him in the kennel in the midst of the dogs.

"His son died in the same fashion in a hotel in Paris, while on a journey in 1841, after having been deceived by an opera singer.

"He left a child of eleven years and a widow, the sister of my moher. She came with the little one to live at my father's house on the De Bertillon estate. I was then seventeen.

"You could not imagine what an astonishing, precocious child this little Santèze was. One would have said that all the powers of tenderness, all the exaltation of his race, had fallen upon this one, the last. He was always dreaming and walking alone in a great avenue of elms that led from the house to the woods. I often watched this sentimental youngster from my window as he walked up and down with his hands behind his back, with bowed head, sometimes stopping to look up, as if he saw and comprehended things beyond his age and experience.

"Often after dinner, on clear nights, he would say to me: 'Let us go and dream, Cousin.' And we would go together into the park. He would stop abruptly in the clear spaces where the white vapor floats, that soft light with which the moon lights up the clearings in the woods, and say to me, seizing my hands: 'Look! Look there! But you do not understand; I feel it. If you comprehended you would be happy. One must know how to love.' I would laugh and embrace him, this boy, who loved me until his dying day.

"Often, too, after dinner he would seat himself upon my mother's knee. 'Come, Aunt,' he would say to her, 'tell us some love story.' And my mother, for his pleasure, would tell him all the family legends, the passionate adventures of his fathers, as they had been told a thousand times, true and false. It is these stories that have ruined these men; they never concealed anything and prided themselves upon not allowing a descendant of their house to lie.

"He would be uplifted, this little one, by these terrible or affecting tales, and sometimes he would clap his hands and cry out: 'I, too; I, too, know how to love, better than any of them.'

"Then he began to pay me his court, a timid, profoundly tender devotion, so droll that one could but laugh at it. Each morning I had flowers picked by him, and each evening, before going to his room, he would kiss my hand, murmuring: 'I love you!'

"I was guilty, very guilty, and I have wept since, unceasingly, doing penance all my life by remaining an old maid—or rather an affianced widow, his widow. I amused myself with this childish devotion, even inciting him. I was coquettish, enticing as if he were a man, caressing and deceiving. I excited this child. It was a joke to me and a pleasing diversion to his mother and mine. He was eleven years old! Think of it! Who would have taken seriously this passion of a midget! I kissed him as much as he wished. I even wrote sweet letters to him that our mothers read. And he responded with letters of fire that I still have. He had a belief all his own in our intimacy and love, judging himself a man. We had forgotten that he was a Santèze!

"This lasted nearly a year. One evening in the park he threw himself down at my knees, kissing the hem of my dress with furious earnestness, repeating: 'I love you! I love you! I love you and shall even to death. If you ever deceive me, understand, if you ever leave me for another, I shall do as my father did.' And he added in a low voice that gave one the shivers: 'You know what I shall do!'

"Then as I remained amazed and dumbfounded, he got up and, stretching himself on tiptoe, for I was much taller than he, he repeated in my ear my name, my first name, 'Genevieve!' in a voice so sweet, so pretty, so tender, that I trembled to my very feet.

"I muttered: 'Let us return to the house!' He said nothing further but followed me. As we were ascending the steps he stopped me and said: 'You know if you abandon me I shall kill myself.'

"I understood now that I had gone too far and immediately became more reserved. When he reproached me for it one day I answered him: 'You are now too large for this kind of joking and too young for serious love. I will wait.'

"I believed myself freed from him.

"He was sent away to school in the autumn. When he returned the following summer I had become engaged. He understood at once and for over a week preserved so calm an appearance that I was much disturbed.

"The ninth day, in the morning, I perceived on rising a little paper slipped under my door. I seized it and read: 'You have abandoned me, and you know what I said. You have ordered my death. As I do not wish to be found by anyone but you, come into the park at the place where last year I said that I loved you, and look up.'

"I felt myself becoming mad. I dressed quickly and ran quickly, so quickly that I fell exhausted at the designated spot. His little school cap was on the ground in the mud. It had rained all night. I raised my eyes and saw something concealed by the leaves, for there was a wind blowing, a strong wind.

"After that I knew nothing of what I did. I shouted, fainted, perhaps, and fell, then got up and ran to the house. I recovered my reason in my bed, with any mother for my pillow.

"I at first believed that I had dreamed all this in a frightful delirium. I muttered: 'And he, he–Gontran, where is he—'

"Then they told me it was all true. I dared not look at him again, but I asked for a lock of his blond hair. Here– it–is." And the old lady held out her hand in a gesture of despair.

Then after much use of her handkerchief and drying of her eyes she continued: "I broke off my engagement without saying why–and I–have remained always the–

widow of this child thirteen years old."

Then her head fell upon her breast, and she wept pensively for a long time.

And as they dispersed to their rooms for the night, a great hunter, whose quiet she had disturbed somewhat, whispered in the ear of his neighbor:

"What a misfortune to be so sentimental! Don't you think so?"

A CRISIS

A BIG FIRE WAS BURNING, and the tea table was set for two. The Count de Sallure threw his hat, gloves and fur coat on a chair, while the countess, who had removed her opera cloak, was smiling amiably at herself in the glass and arranging a few stray curls with her jeweled fingers. Her husband had been looking at her for the past few minutes, as if on the point of saying something, but hesitating; finally he said:

"You have flirted outrageously tonight!" She looked him straight in the eyes with an expression of triumph and defiance on her face.

"Why, certainly," she answered. She sat down, poured out the tea, and her husband took his seat opposite her.

"It made me look quite—ridiculous!"

"Is this a scene?" she asked, arching her brows. "Do you mean to criticize my conduct?"

"Oh no, I only meant to say that Monsieur Burel's attentions to you were positively improper, and if I had the right—I—would not tolerate it."

"Why, my dear boy, what has come over you? You must have changed your views since last year. You did not seem to mind who courted me and who did not a year ago. When I found out that you had a mistress, a mistress whom you loved passionately, I pointed out to you then, as you did me tonight (but I had good reasons), that you were compromising yourself and Madame de Servy, that your conduct grieved me and made me look ridiculous;

what did you answer me? That I was perfectly free, that marriage between two intelligent people was simply a partnership, a sort of social bond, but not a moral bond. Is it not true? You gave me to understand that your mistress was far more captivating than I, that she was more womanly; that is what you said: 'more womanly.' Of course you said all this in a very nice way, and I acknowledge that you did your very best to spare my feelings, for which I am very grateful to you, I assure you, but I understand perfectly what you meant.

"We then decided to live practically separated; that is, under the same roof but apart from each other. We had a child, and it was necessary to keep up appearances before the world, but you intimated that if I chose to take a lover you would not object in the least, providing it was kept secret. You even made a long and very interesting discourse on the cleverness of women in such cases; how well they could manage such things, etc., etc. I understood perfectly, my dear boy. You loved Madame de Servy very much at that time, and my conjugal—legal—affection was an impediment to your happiness, but since then we have lived on the very best of terms. We go out in society together, it is true, but here in our own house we are complete strangers. Now for the past month or two you act as if you were jealous, and I do not understand it."

"I am not jealous, my dear, but you are so young, so impulsive, that I am afraid you will expose yourself to the world's criticisms."

"You make me laugh! Your conduct would not bear a very close scrutiny. You had better not preach what you do not practice."

"Do not laugh, I pray. This is no laughing matter. I am speaking as a friend, a true friend. As to your remarks, they are very much exaggerated."

"Not at all. When you confessed to me your infatuation for Madame de Servy, I took it for granted that you authorized me to imitate you. I have not done so."

"Allow me to—"

"Do not interrupt me. I have not done so. I have no lover--as yet. I am looking for one, but I have not found one to suit me. He must be very nice-nicer than you are--that is a compliment, but you do not seem to appreciate it."

"This joking is entirely uncalled for."

"I am not joking at all; I am in dead earnest. I have not forgotten a single word of what you said to me a year ago, and when it pleases me to do so, no matter what you may say or do, I shall take a lover. I shall do it without your even suspecting it--you will be none the wise--like a great many others."

"How can you say such things?"

"How can I say such things? But, my dear boy, you were the first one to laugh when Madame de Gers joked about poor, unsuspecting Monsieur de Servy."

"That might be, but it is not becoming language for you."

"Indeed! You thought it a good joke when it concerned Monsieur de Servy, but you do not find it so appropriate when it concerns you. What a queer lot men are! However, I am not fond of talking about such things; I simply mentioned it to see if you were ready."

"Ready--for what?"

"Ready to be deceived. When a man gets angry on hearing such things he is not quite ready. I wager that in two months you will be the first one to laugh if I mention a deceived husband to you. It is generally the case when you are the deceived one."

"Upon my word, you are positively rude tonight; I have never seen you that way."

"Yes—I have changed—for the worse, but it is your fault."

"Come, my dear, let us talk seriously. I beg of you, I implore you not to let Monsieur Burel court you as he did tonight."

"You are jealous; I knew it."

"No, no, but I do not wish to be looked upon with ridicule, and if I catch that man devouring you with his eyes like he did tonight—I—I will thrash him!"

"Could it be possible that you are in love with me?"

"Why not? I am sure I could do much worse."

"Thanks. I am sorry for you—because I do not love you any more."

The count got up, walked around the tea table and, going behind his wife, he kissed her quickly on the neck. She sprang up and with flashing eyes said: "How dare you do that? Remember, we are absolutely nothing to each other; we are complete strangers."

"Please do not get angry; I could not help it; you look so lovely tonight."

"Then I must have improved wonderfully."

"You look positively charming; your arms and shoulders are beautiful, and your skin—"

"Would captivate Monsieur Burel."

"How mean you are! But really, I do not recall ever having seen a woman as captivating as you are."

"You must have been fasting lately."

"What's that?"

"I say, you must have been fasting lately."

"Why—what do you mean?"

"I mean just what I say. You must have fasted for some

time, and now you are famished. A hungry man will eat things which he will not eat at any other time. I am the neglected-dish, which you would not mind tonight."

"Marguerite! Whoever taught you to say those things?"

"You did. To my knowledge you have had four mistresses. Actresses, society women, gay women, etc., so how can I explain your sudden fancy for me, except by your long fast?"

"You will think me rude, brutal, but I have fallen in love with you for the second time. I love you madly!"

"Well, well! Then you—wish to—"

"Exactly."

"Tonight?"

"Oh, Marguerite!"

"There, you are scandalized again. My dear boy, let us talk quietly. We are strangers, are we not? I am your wife, it is true, but I am—free. I intended to engage my affection elsewhere, but I will give you the preference, providing—I receive the same compensation."

"I do not understand you; what do you mean?"

"I will speak more clearly. Am I as good looking at your mistresses?"

"A thousand times better."

"Better than the nicest one?"

"Yes, a thousand times."

"How much did she cost you in three months?"

"Really—what on earth do you mean?"

"I mean, how much did you spend on the costliest of your mistresses, in jewelry, carriages, suppers, etc., in three months?"

"How do I know?"

"You ought to know. Let us say, for instance, five thousand francs a month—is that about right?"

"Yes—about that."

"Well, my dear boy, give me five thousand francs and I will be yours for a month, beginning from tonight."

"Marguerite! Are you crazy?"

"No, I am not, but just as you say. Good night!"

The countess entered her boudoir. A vague perfume permeated the whole room. The count appeared in the doorway.

"How lovely it smells in here!"

"Do you think so? I always use Peau d'Espagne; I never use any other perfume."

"Really? I did not notice—it is lovely."

"Possibly, but be kind enough to go; I want to go to bed."

"Marguerite!"

"Will you please go?"

The count came in and sat on a chair.

Said the countess: "You will not go? Very well."

She slowly took off her waist, revealing her white arms and neck, then she lifted her arms above her head to loosen her hair.

The count took a step toward her.

The countess: "Do not come near me or I shall get real angry, do you hear?"

He caught her in his arms and tried to kiss her. She quickly took a tumbler of perfumed water standing on the toilet table and dashed it into his face.

He was terribly angry. He stepped back a few paces and murmured:

"How stupid of you!"

"Perhaps—but you know my conditions—five thousand francs!"

"Preposterous!"

"Why, pray?"

"Why? Because—whoever heard of a man paying his wife?"

"Oh! How horribly rude you are!"

"I suppose I am rude, but I repeat, the idea of paying one's wife is preposterous! Positively stupid!"

"Is it not much worse to pay a gay woman? It certainly would be stupid when you have a wife at home."

"That may be, but I do not wish to be ridiculous."

The countess sat down on the bed and took off her stockings, revealing her bare, pink feet.

The count approached a little nearer and said tenderly:

"What an odd idea of yours, Marguerite!"

"What idea?"

"To ask me for five thousand francs!"

"Odd? Why should it be odd? Are we not strangers? You say you are in love with me; all well and good. You cannot marry me, as I am already your wife, so you buy me. *Mon Dieu!* Have you not bought other women? Is it not much better to give me that money than to a strange woman who would squander it? Come, you will acknowledge that it is a novel idea to actually pay your own wife! An intelligent man like you ought to see how amusing it is; besides, a man never really loves anything unless it costs him a lot of money. It would add new zest to our—conjugal love, by comparing it with your—illegitimate love. Am I not right?"

She went toward the bell.

"Now then, sir, if you do not go I will ring for my maid!"

The count stood perplexed, displeased, and suddenly taking a handful of bank notes out of his pocket, he threw them at his wife, saying:

"Here are six thousand, you witch, but remember—"
The countess picked up the money, counted it and said:
"What?"
"You must not get used to it."
She burst out laughing and said to him:
"Five thousand francs each month, or else I shall send you back to your actresses, and if you are pleased with me—I shall ask for more."

A NORMANDY JOKE

THE PROCESSION came in sight in the hollow road which was shaded by the tall trees which grew on the slopes of the farm. The newly married couple came first, then the relations, then the invited guests and lastly the poor of the neighborhood, while the village urchins, who hovered about the narrow road like flies, ran in and out of the ranks or climbed up the trees to see it better.

The bridegroom was a good-looking young fellow, Jean Patu, the richest farmer in the neighborhood. Above all things he was an ardent sportsman who seemed to lose all common sense in order to satisfy that passion, who spent large sums on his dogs, his keepers, his ferrets and his guns. The bride, Rosalie Roussel, had been courted by all the likely young fellows in the district, for they all thought her prepossessing and they knew that she would have a good dowry, but she had chosen Patu—partly, perhaps, because she liked him better than she did the others, but still more, like a careful Normandy girl, because he had more crown pieces.

When they went in at the white gateway of the husband's farm forty shots resounded without anyone seeing those who fired. The shooters were hidden in the ditches, and the noise seemed to please the men, who were sprawling about heavily in their best clothes, very much. Patu left his wife, and running up to a farm servant whom he perceived behind a tree, he seized his gun and fired a shot himself, kicking his heels about like a colt. Then they went on, beneath the apple trees heavy with fruit, through the high grass and through the herd of calves, who looked at them with their great eyes, got up slowly and remained standing with their muzzles turned toward the wedding party.

The men became serious when they came within measurable distance of the wedding dinner. Some of them, the rich ones, had on tall, shining silk hats, which seemed altogether out of place there; others had old head coverings with a long nap, which might have been taken for moleskin, while the humbler among them wore caps. All the women had shawls on, which they wore as loose wraps, holding the ends daintily under their arms. They were red, particolored, flaming shawls, and their brightness seemed to astonish the black fowls on the dung heap, the ducks on the side of the pond and the pigeons on the thatched roofs.

The extensive farm buildings awaited the party at the end of that archway of apple trees, and a sort of vapor came out of open door and windows, an almost overwhelming smell of eatables, which permeated the vast building, issuing from its openings and even from its very walls. The string of guests extended through the yard; when the foremost of them reached the house they broke the chain and dispersed, while behind they were still coming in at the open gate. The ditches were now lined with urchins and poor curious people. The shots did not cease but came from every side at once, injecting a cloud of smoke, and that powdery smell which has the same intoxicating effects as absinthe, into the atmosphere.

The women were shaking their dresses outside the door to get rid of the dust, were undoing their cap strings and folding their shawls over their arms. Then they went into the house to lay them aside altogether for the time. The table was laid in the great kitchen, which could hold a hundred persons; they sat down to dinner at two o'clock and at eight o'clock they were still eating; the men, in their shirt sleeves, with their waistcoats unbuttoned and with red faces, were swallowing the food and drink as if they were insatiable. The cider sparkled merrily, clear and golden in the large glasses, by the side of the dark, blood-colored wine; and between every dish they made the *trou*, the Normandy *trou*, with a glass of brandy which inflamed the body and put foolish notions into the head.

From time to time one of the guests, being as full as a barrel, would go out for a few moments to get a mouthful of fresh air as they said, and then return with redoubled appetite. The farmers' wives, with scarlet faces and their corsets nearly bursting, did not like to follow their example, until one of them, feeling more uncomfortable than the others, went out. Then all the rest followed her example and came back quite ready for any fun, and the rough jokes began afresh. Broadsides of doubtful jokes were exchanged across the table, all about the wedding night, until the whole arsenal of peasant wit was exhausted. For the last hundred years the same broad jokes had served for similar occasions, and although everyone knew them, they still hit the mark and made both rows of guests roar with laughter.

At the bottom of the table four young fellows, who were neighbors, were preparing some practical jokes for the newly married couple, and they seemed to have got hold of a good one by the way they whispered and laughed. Suddenly one of them, profiting by a moment of silence, exclaimed: "The poachers will have a good time tonight with this moon! I say, Jean, you will not be looking at the moon, will you?" The bridegroom turned to him quickly and replied: "Only let them come, that's all!" But the other young fellow began to laugh and said: "I do not think you will neglect your duty for them!"

The whole table was convulsed with laughter, so that the glasses shook, but the bridegroom became furious at the thought that anybody should profit by his wedding to come and poach on his land and repeated: "I only say: just let them come!"

Then there was a flood of talk with a double meaning which made the bride blush somewhat, although she was trembling with expectation, and when they had emptied the kegs of brandy they all went to bed. The young couple went into their own room, which was on the ground floor as most rooms in farmhouses are. As it was very warm they opened the windows and closed the shutters. A small lamp in bad taste, a present from the bride's father, was burning on the chest of drawers, and the bed stood ready to receive the young people, who did not stand upon all the ceremony which is usual among refined people.

The young woman had already taken off her wreath and her dress and was in her petticoat, unlacing her boots, while Jean was finishing his cigar and looking at her out of the corners of his eyes. It was an ardent look, more sensual than tender, for he felt more desire than love for her. Suddenly, with a brusque movement, like a man who is going to set to work, he took off his coat. She had already taken off her boots and was now pulling off her stockings; then she said to him: "Go and hide yourself behind the curtains while I get into bed."

He seemed as if he were going to refuse but with a cunning look went and hid himself with the exception of his head. She laughed and tried to cover up his eyes, and they romped in an amorous and happy manner, without shame or embarrassment. At last he did as she asked him, and in a moment she unfastened her petticoat, which slipped down her legs, fell at her feet and lay on the floor in a circle. She left it there, stepped over it, naked with the exception of her floating chemise, and slipped into the bed, whose springs creaked beneath her weight. He immediately went up to her, without his shoes and in his trousers, and, stooping over his wife, sought her lips, which she hid beneath the pillow, when a shot was heard in the distance, in the direction of the forest of Râpées, as he thought.

He raised himself anxiously, and running to the window, with his heart beating, he opened the shutters. The full moon flooded the yard with yellow light, and the silhouettes of the apple trees made black shadow at his feet, while in the distance the fields gleamed, covered with the ripe corn. But as he was leaning out, listening to every sound in the still night, two bare arms were put around his neck, and his wife whispered, trying to pull him back. "Do leave them alone; it has nothing to do with you. Come to bed."

He turned round, put his arms round her and drew her toward him, feeling her warm skin through the thin material, and lifting her up in his vigorous arms, he carried her toward their couch; but just as he was laying her on the bed, which yielded beneath her weight, they heard another report, considerably nearer this time. Jean, giving way to his tumultuous age, swore aloud: "Good God! Do you think, I shall not go out and see what it is because of you? Wait, wait a few minutes!" He put on his shoes again, took down his gun, which was always hanging within reach upon the wall, and, as his wife threw herself on her knees in her terror to implore him not to go, he hastily freed himself, ran to the window and jumped into the yard.

She waited one hour, two hours, until daybreak, but her husband did not return. Then she lost her head, aroused the house, related how angry Jean was and said that he had gone after the poachers, and immediately all the male farm servants, even the boys, went in search of their master. They found him two leagues from the farm, tied hand and foot, half dead with rage, his gun broken, his trousers turned inside out, three dead hares hanging round his neck and a placard on his chest with these words:

Who goes on the chase loses his place.

And later on when he used to tell this story of his wedding night he generally added: "Ah! As far as a joke went, it was a good joke. They caught me in a snare, as if I had been a rabbit, the dirty brutes, and they shoved my head into a bag. But if I can only catch them someday, they had better look out for themselves!"

That is how they amuse themselves in Normandy on a wedding day.

USELESS BEAUTY

A VERY ELEGANT VICTORIA with two beautiful black horse was drawn up in front of the mansion. It was a day in the latter and of June about half-past five in the afternoon, and the sun shone warm and bright into the large courtyard.

The Countess de Mascaret came down just as her husband, who was coming home, appeared in the carriage entrance. He stopped for a few moments to look at his wife and grew rather pale. She was very beautiful, graceful and distinguished looking with her long oval face, her complexion like gilt ivory, her large gray eyes and her black hair, and she got into her carriage without looking at him, without even seeming to have noticed him, with such a particularly highbred air that the furious jealousy by which he had been devoured for so long again gnawed at his heart. He went up to her and said. "You are going for a drive?"

She merely replied disdainfully: "You see I am!"

"In the Bois de Boulogne?"

"Most probably."

"May I come with you?"

"The carriage belongs to you."

Without being surprised at the tone of voice in which she answered him, he got in and sat down by his wife's side and said: "Bois de Boulogne." The footman jumped up by the coachman's side, and the horses, as usual, pawed the ground and shook their heads until they were in the street. Husband and wife sat side by side without speaking. He was thinking how to begin a conversation, but she maintained such an obstinately hard look that he did not venture to make the attempt. At last, however, he cunningly, accidentally as it were, touched the countess's gloved hand with his own, but she drew her arm away with a movement which was so expressive of disgust that he remained thoughtful in spite of his usual authoritative and despotic character. "Gabrielle!" he said at last.

"What do you want?"

"I think you are looking adorable."

She did not reply but remained lying back in the carriage, looking like an irritated queen. By that time they were driving up the Champs Elysées, toward the Arc de Triomphe. That immense monument at the end of the long avenue raised its colossal arch against the red sky, and the sun seemed to be sinking onto it, showering fiery dust on it from the sky.

The stream of carriages, with the sun reflecting from the bright, plated harness and the shining lamps, were like a double current flowing, one toward the town and one toward the wood, and the Count de Mascaret continued: "My dear Gabrielle!"

Then, unable to bear it any longer, she replied in an exasperated voice:

"Oh, do leave me in peace, pray! I am not even at liberty to have my carriage to myself now." He, however, pretended not to hear her and continued: "You have never looked so pretty as you do today."

Her patience was decidedly at an end, and she replied with irrepressible anger: "You are wrong to notice it, for I swear to you that I will never have anything to do with you in that way again." He was stupefied and agitated and, his violent nature gaining the upper hand, he exclaimed: "What do you mean by that?" in such a manner as revealed rather the brutal master than the amorous man. But she replied in a low voice so that the servants might not hear amid the deafening noise of the wheels:

"Ah! What do I mean by that? What do I mean by that? Now I recognize you again! Do you want me to tell everything?"

"Yes."

"Everything that has been on my heart since I have been the victim of your terrible selfishness?"

He had grown red with surprise and anger, and he growled between his closed teeth: "Yes, tell me everything."

He was a tall, broad-shouldered man, with a big red beard, a handsome man, a nobleman, a man of the world, who passed as a perfect husband and an excellent father, and now for the first time since they had started she turned toward him and looked him full in the face. "Ah! You will hear some disagreeable things, but you must know that I am prepared for everything, that I fear nothing, and you less than anyone today."

He also was looking into her eyes and already was shaking with passion; then he said in a low voice: "You are mad."

"No, but I will no longer be the victim of the hateful penalty of maternity which you have inflicted on me for eleven years! I wish to live like a woman of the world, as I have the right to do, as all women have the right to do."

He suddenly grew pale again and stammered: "I do not understand you."

"Oh yes; you understand me well enough. It is now three months since I had my last child, and as I am still very beautiful, and as, in spite of all your efforts, you cannot spoil my figure, as you just now perceived when you saw me on the outside flight of steps, you think it is time that I should become *enceinte* again."

"But you are talking nonsense!"

"No, I am not; I am thirty and I have had seven children, and we have been married eleven years, and you hope that this will go on for ten years longer, after which you will leave off being jealous."

He seized her arm and squeezed it, saying: "I will not allow you to talk to me like that for long."

"And I shall talk to you till the end, until I have finished all I have to say to you, and if you try to prevent me I shall raise my voice so that the two servants who are on the box may hear. I only allowed you to come with me for that object, for I have these witnesses, who will oblige you to listen to me and to contain yourself; so now pay attention to what I say. I have always felt an antipathy for you and I have always let you see it, for I have never lied, monsieur. You married me in spite of myself; you forced my parents, who were in embarrassed circumstances, to give me to you because you were rich, and they obliged me to marry you, in spite of my tears.

"So you bought me, and as soon as I was in your power, as soon as I had become your companion, ready to attach myself to you, to forget your coercive and threatening proceedings, in order that I might only remember that I ought to be a devoted wife and to love you as much as it might be possible for me to love you, you became jealous— you—as no man has ever been before, with the base, ignoble jealousy of a spy, which was as degrading for you as it was for me. I had not been married eight months when you suspected me of every perfidiousness, and you even told me so. What a disgrace! And as you could not prevent me from being beautiful and from pleasing people, from being called in drawing rooms and also in the newspapers one of the most beautiful women in Paris; you tried everything you could think of to keep admirers from me and you hit upon the abominable idea of making me spend my life in a constant state of motherhood, until the time when I should disgust every man. Oh, do not deny it! I did not understand it for some time, but then I guessed it. You even boasted about it to your sister, who told me of it, for she is fond of me and was disgusted at your boorish coarseness.

"Ah! Remember our struggles, doors smashed in and locks forced! For eleven years you have condemned me to the existence of a brood mare. Then as soon as I was pregnant you grew disgusted with me, and I saw nothing of you for months and I was sent into the country to the family mansion, among fields and meadows, to bring forth my child. And when I reappeared, fresh, pretty and indestructible, still seductive and constantly surrounded by admirers, hoping that at last I should live a little like a young rich woman who belongs to society, you were seized by jealousy again, and you recommenced to persecute me with that infamous and hateful desire from which you are suffering at this moment by my side. And it is not the desire of possessing me–for I should never have refused myself to you–but it is the wish to make me unsightly.

"Besides this, that abominable and mysterious circumstance took place which I was a long time in penetrating (but I grew acute by dint of watching your thoughts and actions). You atached yourself to your children with all the security which they gave you while I bore them in my womb. You felt affection for them with all your aversion for me and in spite of your ignoble fears, which were momentarily allayed by your pleasure in seeing me a mother.

"Oh! How often have I noticed that joy in you! I have seen it in your eyes and guessed it. You loved your children as victories and not because they were of your own blood. They were victories over me, over my youth, over my beauty, over my charms, over the compliments which were paid me and over those who whispered round me, without paying them to me. And you are proud of them; you make a parade of them; you take them out for drives in your coach in the Bois de Boulogne, and you give them donkey rides at Montmorency. You take them to theatrical matinees so that you may be seen in the midst of them and that people may say: 'What a kind father!' and that it may be repeated."

He had seized her wrist with savage brutality and squeezed it so violently that she was quiet, though she nearly cried out with the pain. Then he said to her in a whisper:

"I love my children; do you hear? What you have just told me is disgraceful in a mother. But you belong to me; I am master—your master. I can exact from you what I like and when I like—and I have the law on my side."

He was trying to crush her fingers in the strong grip of his large, muscular hand, and she, livid with pain, tried in vain to free them from that vise which was crushing them; the agony made her pant, and the tears came into her eyes. "You see that I am the master and the stronger," he said. And when he somewhat loosened his grip she asked him: "Do you think that I am a religious woman?"

He was surprised and stammered: "Yes."

"Do you think that I could lie if I swore to the truth of

anything to you before an altar on which Christ's body is?"

"No."

"Will you go with me to some church?"

"What for?"

"You shall see. Will you?"

"If you absolutely wish it, yes."

She raised her voice and said: "Philip!" And the coachman, bending down a little, without taking his eyes from his horses, seemed to turn his ear alone toward his mistress, who said: "Drive to St Philip-du-Roule's." And the victoria, which had reached the entrance of the Bois de Boulogne, returned to Paris.

Husband and wife did not exchange a word during the drive. When the carriage stopped before the church Countess de Mascaret jumped out and entered it, followed by the count a few yards behind her. She went without stopping as far as the choir screen and, falling on her knees at a chair, she buried her face in her hands. She prayed for a long time, and he, standing behind her, could see that she was crying. She wept noiselessly, like women do weep when they are in great and poignant grief. There was a kind of undulation in her body, which ended in a little sob, hidden and stifled by her fingers.

But Count de Mascaret thought that the situation was long drawn out, and he touched her on the shoulder. That contact recalled her to herself, as if she had been burned, and, getting up, she looked straight into his eyes.

"This is what I have to say to you. I am afraid of nothing, whatever you may do to me. You may kill me if you like. One of your children is not yours, and one only; that I swear to you before God who hears me here. That is the only revenge which was possible for me in return for all your abominable male tyrannies, in return for the penal servitude of childbearing to which you have condemned me. Who was my lover? That you will never know! You may suspect everyone, but you will never find out. I gave myself up to him without love and without pleasure, only for the sake of betraying you and he made me a mother. Which is his child? That also you will never know. I have seven; try and find out! I intended to tell you this later, for one cannot completely avenge oneself on a man by deceiving him, unless he knows it. You have driven me to confess it today; now I have finished."

She hurried through the church toward the open door, expecting to hear behind her the quick steps of her husband whom she had defied and to be knocked to the ground by a blow of his fist, but she heard nothing and reached her carriage. She jumped into it at a bound, overwhelmed with anguish and breathless with fear; she called out to the coachman, "Home!" and the horses set off at a quick trot.

II

The Countess de Mascaret was waiting in her room for dinnertime, like a criminal sentenced to death awaits the hour of his execution. What was he going to do? Had he come home? Despotic, passionate, ready for any violence as he was, what was he meditating; what had he made up his mind to do? There was no sound in the house, and every moment she looked at the clock. Her maid had come and dressed her for the evening and had then left the room again. Eight o'clock struck; almost at the same moment there were two knocks at the door, and the butler came in and told her that dinner was ready.

"Has the count come in?"

"Yes, Madame la Comtesse; he is in the dining room."

For a moment she felt inclined to arm herself with a small revolver which she had bought some weeks before, foreseeing the tragedy which was being rehearsed in her heart. But she remembered that all the children would be there, and she took nothing except a smelling bottle. He rose somewhat ceremoniously from his chair. They exchanged a slight bow and sat down. The three boys with their tutor, Abbé Martin, were on her right, and the three girls with Miss Smith, their English governess, were on her left. The youngest child, who was only three months old, remained upstairs with his nurse.

The abbé said grace, as was usual when there was no comapany, for the children did not come down to dinner when there were guests present; then they began dinner. The countess, suffering from emotion which she had not at all calculated upon, remained with her eyes cast down, while the count scrutinized now the three boys and now the three girls with uncertain, unhappy looks, which traveled from one to the other. Suddenly, pushing his wineglass from him, it broke, and the wine was spilt on the tablecloth, and at the slight noise caused by this little accident the countess started up from her chair, and for the first time they looked at each other. Then almost every moment, in spite of themselves, in spite of the irritation of their nerves caused by every glance, they did not cease to exchange looks, rapid as pistol shots.

The abbé, who felt that there was some cause for embarrassment which he could not divine, tried to get up a conversation and started various subjects, but his useless efforts gave rise to no ideas and did not bring out a word. The countess, with feminine tact and obeying the instincts of a woman of the world, tried to answer him two or three times, but in vain. She could not find words in the perplexity of her mind, and her own voice almost frightened her in the silence of the large room, where nothing else was heard except the slight sound of plates and knives and forks.

Suddenly her husband said to her, bending forward: "Here, amid your children, will you swear to me that what you told me just now is true?"

The hatred which was fermenting in her veins suddenly roused her, and replying to that question with the same firmness with which she had replied to his looks, she raised both her hands, the right pointing toward the boys and the left toward the girls, and said in a firm, resolute voice and without any hesitation: "On the heads of my children, I swear that I have told you the truth."

He got up and, throwing his table napkin onto the table with an exasperated movement, turned round and flung his chair against the wall. Then he went out without another word, while she, uttering a deep sigh, as if after a first victory, went on in a calm voice: "You must not pay any attention to what your father has just said, my darlings; he was very much upset a short time ago, but he will be all right again in a few days."

Then she talked with the abbé and with Miss Smith and had tender, pretty words for all her children, those sweet, spoiling mother's ways which unlock little hearts.

When dinner was over she went into the drawing room with all her little following. She made the elder ones chatter, and when their bedtime came she kissed them for a long time and then went alone into her room.

She waited for she had no doubt that he would come, and she made up her mind then, as her children were not with her, to defend her human flesh, as she defended her life as a woman of the world; and in the pocket of her dress she put the little loaded revolver which she had bought a few weeks before. The hours went by; the hours struck, and every sound was hushed in the house. Only cabs continued to rumble through the streets, but their noise was only heard vaguely through the shuttered and curtained windows.

She waited, energetic and nervous, without any fear of him now, ready for anything and almost triumphant, for she had found means of torturing him continually during every moment of his life.

But the first gleams of dawn came in through the fringe at the bottom of her curtains without his having come into her room, and then she awoke to the fact, much to her surprise, that he was not coming. Having locked and bolted her door for greater security, she went to bed at last and remained there with her eyes open, thinking and barely understanding it all, without being able to guess what he was going to do.

When her maid brought her tea she at the same time gave her a letter from her husband. He told her that he was going to undertake a longish journey, and in a postscript he added that his lawyer would provide her with such money as she might require for her expenses.

III

It was at the opera, between two of the acts in *Robert the Devil*. In the stalls the men were standing up with their hats on, their waistcoats cut very low so as to show a large amount of white shirt front in which the gold and precious stones of their studs glistened. They were looking at the boxes crowded with ladies in low dresses, covered with diamonds and pearls, women who seemed to expand like flowers in that illuminated hothouse, where the beauty of their faces and the whiteness of their shoulders seemed to bloom for inspection in the midst of the music and of human voices.

Two friends with their backs to the orchestra were scanning those parterres of elegance, that exhibition of real or false charms, of jewels, of luxury and of pretension which showed itself off all round the Grand Theater. One of them, Roger de Salnis, said to his companion, Bernard Grandin: "Just look how beautiful Countess de Mascaret still is."

Then the elder, in turn, looked through his opera glasses at a tall lady in a box opposite, who appeared to be still very young and whose striking beauty seemed to appeal to men's eyes in every corner of the house. Her pale complexion, of an ivory tint, gave her the appearance of a statue, while a small diamond coronet glistened on her black hair like a cluster of stars.

When he had looked at her for some time Bernard Grandin replied with a jocular accent of sincere conviction: "You may well call her beautiful!"

"How old do you think she is?"

"Whait a moment. I can tell you exactly, for I have known her since she was a child, and I saw her make her debut into society when she was quite a girl. She is—she is—thirty—thirty-six."

"Impossible!"

"I am sure of it."

"She looks twenty-five."

"She has had seven children."

"It is incredible."

"And what is more, they are all seven alive, as she is a very good mother. I go to the house, which is a very quiet and pleasant one, occasionally, and she presents the phenomenon of the family in the midst of the world."

"How very strange! And have there never been any reports about her?"

"Never."

"But what about her husband? He is peculiar, is he not?"

"Yes and no. Very likely there has been a little drama between them, one of those little domestic dramas which one suspects, which one never finds out exactly, but which one guesses pretty nearly."

"What is it?"

"I do not know anything about it. Mascaret leads a very fast life now, after having been a model husband. As long as he remained a good spouse he had a shocking temper and was crabbed and easily took offense, but since he has been leading his present rackety life he has become quite indifferent, but one would guess that he has some trouble, a worm gnawing somewhere, for he has aged very much."

Thereupon the two friends talked philosophically for some minutes about the secret, unknowable troubles which differences of character or perhaps physical antipathies, which were not perceived at first, give rise to in families. Then Roger de Salnis, who was still looking at Mme de Mascaret through his opera glasses, said:

"It is almost incredible that that woman has had seven children!"

"Yes, in eleven years, after which, when she was thirty, she put a stop to her period of production in order to enter into the brilliant period of entertain, which does not seem near coming to an end."

"Poor women!"

"Why do you pity them?"

"Why? Ah! my dear fellow, just consider! Eleven years of maternity for such a woman! What a hell! All her youth, all her beauty, every hope of success, every poetical ideal of a bright life, sacrificed to that abominable law of reproduction which turns the normal woman into a mere machine for maternity."

"What would you have? It is only nature!"

"Yes, but I say that nature is our enemy, that we must always fight against nature, for she is continually briging us back to an animal state. You may be sure that God has not put anything on this earth that is clean, pretty, elegant or accessory to our ideal, but the human brain has done it. It is we who have introduced a little grace, beauty, unknown charm and mystery into creation by singing about it, interpreting it, by admiring it as poets, idealizing it as artists and by explaining it as learned men who make mistakes, who find ingenious reasons, some grace and beauty, some unknown charm and mystery, in the various phenomena of nature.

"God only created coarse beings, full of the germs of disease, and who, after a few years of bestial enjoyment, grow old and infirm, with all the ugliness and all the want of power of human decrepitude. He only seems to have made them in order that they may reproduce their species in a repulsive manner and then die like ephemeral insects. I said, *reproduce their species in a repulsive manner,* and I adhere to that expression. What is there as a matter of fact, more ignoble and more repugnant than that ridiculous act of the reproduction of living beings, against which all delicate minds always have revolted and always will revolt? Since all the organs which have been invented by this economical and malicious Creator serve two purposes, why did he not choose those that were unsullied, in order to intrust them with that sacred mission, which is the noblest and the most exalted of all human functions? The mouth which nourishes the body by means of material food also diffuses abroad speech and thought. Out flesh revives itself by means of itself, and at the same time ideas are communicated by it. The sense of smell which gives the vital air to the lungs imparts all the perfumes of the world to the brain: the smell of flowers, of woods, of trees, of the sea. The ear which enables us to communicate with our fellow men, has also allowed us to invent music, to create dreams, happiness, the infinite and even physical pleasure by means of sounds!

"But one might say that the Creator wished to prohibit man from ever ennobling and idealizing his commerce with women. Nevertheless, man has found love, which is not a bad reply to that sly Deity, and he has ornamented it so much with literary poetry that woman often forgets the contact she is obliged to submit to. Those among us who are powerless to deceive themselves have invented vice and refined debauchery, which is another way of laughing at 'God and of paying homage, immodest homage, to beauty.

"But the normal man makes children, just a beast that is coupled with another by law.

"Look at that woman! Is it not abominable to think that such a jewel, such a pearl, born to be beautiful, admired, feted and adored, has spent eleven years of her life in providing heirs for the Count de Mascaret?"

Bernard Grandin replied with a laugh: "There is a great deal of truth in all that, but very few people would understand you."

Salnis got more and more animated. "Do you know how I picture God myself?" he said. "As an enormous creative organ unknown to us, who scatters millions of worlds into space, just as one single fish would deposit its spawn in the sea. He creates, because it is His function as God to do so, but He does not know what He is doing and is stupidly prolific in His work and is ignorant of the combinations of all kinds which are produced by His scattered germs. Human thought is a lucky little local, passing accident, which was totally unforeseen and is condemned to disappear with this earth and to recommence perhaps here or elsewhere, the same or different, with fresh combinations of eternally new beginnings. We owe it to this slight accident which has happened to His intellect that we are very uncomfortable in this world which was not made for us, which had not been prepared to receive us, to lodge and feed us or to satisfy reflecting beings, and we owe it to Him also that we have to struggle without ceasing against what are still called the designs of Providence, when we are really refined and civilized beings."

Grandin, who was listening to him attentively, as he had long known the surprising outbursts of his fancy, asked him: "Then you believe that human thought is the spontaneous product of blind, divine parturition?"

"Naturally. A fortuitous function of the nerve centers of our brain, like some unforeseen chemical action which is due to new mixtures and which also resembles a product of electricity, caused by friction or the unexpected proximity of some substance, and which, lastly, resembles the phenomena caused by the infinite and fruitful fermentations of living matter.

"But, my dear fellow, the truth of this must be evident

to anyone who looks about him. If human thought, ordained by an omniscient Creator, had been intended to be what it has become, altogether different from mechanical thoughts and resignation, so exacting, inquiring, agitated, tormented, would the world which was created to receive the beings which we now are have been this unpleasant little dwelling place for poor fools, this salad plot, this rocky, wooded and spherical kitchen garden where your improvident Providence has destined us to live naked in caves or under trees, nourished on the flesh of slaughtered animals, our brethren, or on raw vegetables nourished by the sun and the rain?

"But it is sufficient to reflect for a moment, in order to understand that this world was not made for such creatures as we are. Thought, which is developed by a miracle in the nerves of the cells and our brain, powerless, ignorant and confused as it is, and as it will always remain, makes all of us who are intellectual beings eternal and wretched exiles on earth.

"Look at this earth, as God has given it to those who inhabit it. Is it not visibly and solely made, planted and covered with forests, for the sake of animals? What is there for us? Nothing. And for them? Everything. They have nothing to do but to eat or go hunting and eat each other, according to their instincts, for God never foresaw gentleness and peaceable manners, He only foresaw the death of creatures which were bent on destroying and devouring each other. Are not the quail, the pigeon and the partridge the natural prey of the hawk? The sheep, the stag and the ox that of the great flesh-eating animals, rather than meat that has been fattened to be served up to us with truffles, which have been unearthed by pigs for our special benefit?

"As to ourselves, the more civilized, intellectual and refined we are, the more we ought to conquer and subdue that animal instinct, which represents the will of God in us. And so in order to mitigate our lot as brutes, we have discovered and made everything, beginning with houses, then exquisite food, sauces, sweetmeats, pastry, drink, stuffs, clothes, ornaments, beds, mattresses, carriages, railways and innumerable machines, besides arts and sciences, writing and poetry. Every ideal comes from us as well as the amenities of life, in order to make our existence as simple reproducers, for which divine Providence solely intended us, less monotonous and less hard.

"Look at this theater. Is there not here a human world created by us, unforeseen and unknown by eternal destinies, comprehensible by our minds alone, a sensual and intellectual distraction, which has been invented solely by and for that discontented and restless little animal that we are.

"Look at that woman, Madame de Mascaret. God intended her to live in a cave naked or wrapped up in the skins of wild animals, but is she not better as she is? But speaking of her, does anyone know why and how her brute of a husband, having such a companion by his side and especially after having been boorish enough to make her a mother seven times, has suddenly left her to run after bad women?"

Grandin replied: "Oh, my dear fellow, this is probably the only reason. He found that always living with her was becoming too expensive in the end, and from reasons of domestic economy he has arrived at the same principles which you lay down as a philosopher."

Just then the curtain rose for the third act, and they

turned round, took off their hats and sat down.

IV

The Count and Countess Mascaret were sitting side by side in the carriage which was taking them home from the opera, without speaking. But suddenly the husband said to his wife: "Gabrielle!"

"What do you want?"

"Don't you think that this has lasted long enough?"

"What?"

"The horrible punishment to which you have condemned me for the last six years."

"What do you want? I cannot help it."

"Then tell me which of them it is?"

"Never."

"Think that I can no longer see my children or feel them round me without having my heart burdened with this doubt. Tell me which of them it is, and I swear that I will forgive you and treat it like the others."

"I have not the right to."

"You do not see that I can no longer endure this life, this thought which is wearing me out or this question which I am constantly asking myself, this question which tortures me each time I look at them. It is driving me mad."

"Then you have suffered a great deal?" she said.

"Terribly. Should I, without that, have accepted the horror of living by your side and the still greater horror of feeling and knowing that there is one among them whom I cannot recognize and who prevents me from loving the others?"

She repeated: "Then you have really suffered very much?" And he replied in a constrained and sorrowful voice:

"Yes, for do I not tell you every day that it is intolerable torture to me? Should I have remained in that house near you and them if I did not love them? Oh! You have behaved abominably toward me. All the affection of my heart I have bestowed upon my children, and that you know. I am for them a father of the olden time, as I was for you a husband of one of the families of old, for by instinct I have remained a natural man, a man of former days. Yes, I will confess it, you have made me terribly jealous, because you are a woman of another race, of another soul, with other requirements. Oh! I shall never forget the things that you told me, but from that day I troubled myself no more about you. I did not kill you because then I should have had no means on earth of ever discovering which of our—of your—children is not mine. I have waited but I have suffered more than you would believe, for I can no longer venture to love them, except, perhaps, the two eldest; I no longer venture to look at them, to call them to me, to kiss them; I cannot take them onto my knee without asking myself: 'Can it be this one?' I have been correct in my behavior toward you for six years, and even kind and complaisant; tell me the truth, and I swear that I will do nothing unkind."

He thought, in spite of the darkness of the carriage, that he could perceive that she was moved and, feeling certain that she was going to speak at last, he said: "I beg you, I beseech you, to tell me."

"I have been more guilty than you think perhaps," she replied, "but I could no longer endure that life of continual pregnancy, and I had only one means of driving you from my bed. I lied before God, and I lied with my hand raised to my children's heads, for I have never wronged you."

He seized her arm in the darkness and, squeezing it as

he had done on that terrible day of their drive in the Bois de Boulogne, he stammered: "Is that true?"

"It is true."

But he in terrible grief said with a groan: "I shall have fresh doubts that will never end! When did you lie, the last time or now? How am I to believe you at present? How can one believe a woman after that? I shall never again know what I am to think. I would rather you had said to me: 'It is Jacques,' or, 'It is Jeanne.'"

The carriage drove them into the courtyard of their mansion, and when it had drawn up in front of the steps the count got down first, as usual, and offered his wife his arm to help her up. And then as soon as they had reached the first floor he said: "May I speak to you for a few moments longer?"

And she replied: "I am quite willing."

They went into a small drawing room, while a footman in some surprise lit the wax candles. As soon as he had left the room and they were alone he continued: "How am I to know the truth? I have begged you a thousand times to speak, but you have remained dumb, impenetrable, inflexible, inexorable, and now today you tell me that you have been lying. For six years you have actually allowed me to believe such a thing! No, you are lying now; I do not know why, but out of pity for me perhaps?"

She replied in a sincere and convincing manner: "If I had not done so I should have had four more children in the last six years!"

And he exclaimed: "Can a mother speak like that?"

"Oh!" she replied. "I do not at all feel that I am the mother of children who have never been born; it is enough for me to be the mother of those that I have and to love them with all my heart. I am—we are—women who belong to the civilized world, monsieur, and we are no longer, and we refuse to be, mere females who restock the earth."

She got up, but he seized here hands. "Only one word, Gabrielle. Tell me the truth!"

"I have just told you. I have never dishonored you."

He looked her full in the face, and how beautiful she was, with her gray eyes, like the cold sky. In her dark hairdress, on that opaque night of black hair, there shone the diamond coronet, like a cluster of stars. Then he suddenly felt, felt by a kind of intuition, that this grand creature was not merely a being destined to perpetuate his race, but the strange and mysterious product of all the complicated desires which have been accumulating in us for centuries but which have been turned aside from their primitive and divine object and which have wandered after a mystic, imperfectly seen and intangible beauty. There are some women like that, women who blossom only for our dreams, adorned with every poetical attribute of civilization, with that ideal luxury, coquetry and esthetic charm which should surround the living statue who brightens our life.

Her husband remained standing before her, stupefied at the tardy and obscure discovery, confusedly hitting on the cause of his former jealousy and understanding it all very imperfectly. At last he said: "I believe you, for I feel at this moment that you are not lying, and formerlyI really thought that you were."

She put out her hand to him: "We are friends then?"

He took her hand and kissed it and replied: "We are friends. Thank you, Gabrielle."

Then he went out, still looking at her and surprised that she was still so beautiful and feeling a strange emotion arising in him which was, perhaps, more formidable than antique and simple love.

MADAME TELLIER'S EXCURSION

MEN WENT there every evening at about eleven o'clock, just as they went to the café. Six or eight of them used to meet there, always the same set—not fast men, but respectable tradesmen and young men in government or some other employ—and they used to drink their chartreuse and tease the girls, or else they would talk seriously with Madame, whom everybody respected, and then would go home at twelve o'clock. The younger men would sometimes stay the night.

It was a small, comfortable house at the corner of a street behind St. Etienne's Church. From the windows one could see the docks, full of ships which were being unloaded, and on the hill the old gray chapel, dedicated to the Virgin.

Madame, who came of a respectable family of peasant proprietors in the department of the Eure, had taken up her profession, just as she would have become a milliner or dressmaker. The prejudice against prostitution, which is so violent and deeply rooted in large towns, does not exist in the country places in Normandy. The peasant simply says: "It is a paying business," and sends his daughter to keep a harem of fast girls, just as he would send her to keep a girls' school.

She had inherited the house from an old uncle to whom it had belonged. Monsieur and Madame, who had formerly been innkeepers near Yvetot, had immediately sold their house, as they thought that the business at Fécamp was more profitable. They arrived one fine morning to assume the direction of the enterprise, which was declining on account of the absence of a head. They were good enough people in their way and soon made themselves liked by their staff and their neighbors.

Monsieur died of apoplexy two years later, for as his new profession kept him in idleness and without exercise, he had grown excessively stout, and his health had suffered. Since Madame had been a widow, all the frequenters of the establishment had wanted her, but people said that personally she was quite virtuous, and even the girls in the house could not discover anything against her. She was tall, stout and affable, and her complexion, which had become pale in the dimness of her house, the shutters of which were scarcely ever opened, shone as if it had been varnished. She had a fringe of curly false hair, which gave her a juvenile look, which in turn contrasted strongly with her matronly figure. She was always smiling and cheerful and was fond of a joke, but there was a shade of reserve about her which her new occupation had not quite made her lose. Coarse words always shocked her, and when any young fellow who had been badly brought up called her establishment by its right name, she was angry and disgusted.

In a word, she had a refined mind, and although she treated her women as friends, yet she very frequently used to say that she and they were not made of the same stuff.

Sometimes during the week she would hire a carriage and take some of her girls into the country, where they used to enjoy themselves on the grass by the side of the little river. They behaved like a lot of girls let out from a school and used to run races and play childish games. They would have a cold dinner on the grass and drink cider and go home at night with a delicious feeling of fatigue and in the carriage kiss Madame as a kind mother who was full of goodness and complaisance.

The house had two entrances. At the corner there was a sort of low café, which sailors and the lower orders frequented at night, and she had two girls whose special duty it was to attend to that part of the business. With the assistance of the waiter, whose name was Frederic and who was a short, light-haired, beardless fellow, as strong as a horse, they set the half bottles of wine and the jugs of beer on the shaky marble tables and then, sitting astride on the customers' knees, would urge them to drink.

The three other girls (there were only five in all) formed a kind of aristocracy and were reserved for the company on the first floor, unless they were wanted downstairs and there was nobody on the first floor. The salon of Jupiter, where the tradesmen used to meet, was papered in blue and embellished with a large drawing representing Leda stretched out under the swan. That room was reached by a winding staircase which ended at a narrow door opening on to the street, and above it all night long a little lamp burned behind wire bars, such as one still sees in some towns at the foot of the shrine of some saint.

The house, which was old and damp, rather smelled of mildew. At times there was an odor of eau de cologne in the passages, or a half-open door downstairs allowed the noise of the common men sitting and drinking downstairs to reach the first floor, much to the disgust of the gentlemen who were there. Madame, who was quite familiar with those of her customers with whom she was on friendly terms, did not leave the salon. She took much interest in what was going on in the town, and they regularly told her all the news. Her serious conversation was a change from the ceaseless chatter of the three women; it was a rest from the doubtful jokes of those stone individuals who every evening indulged in the commonplace amusement of drinking a glass of liquor in company with girls of easy virtue.

The names of the girls on the first floor were Fernande, Raphaelle and Rosa the Jade. As the staff was limited, Madame had endeavored that each member of it should be a pattern, an epitome of each feminine type, so that every coustomer might find as nearly as possible the realization of his ideal. Fernande represented the handsome blonde; she was very tall, rather fat and lazy, a country girl who could not get rid of her freckles and whose short, light, almost colorless, towlike hair, which was like combed-out flax, barely covered her head.

Raphaelle, who came from Marseilles, played the indispensable part of the handsome Jewess. She was thin, with high cheekbones covered with rouge, and her black hair, which was always covered with pomatum, curled onto her forehead. Her eyes would have been handsome if the right one had not had a speck in it. Her Roman nose came down over a square jaw, where two false upper teeth contrasted strangely with the bad color of the rest.

Rosa the Jade was a little roll of fat, nearly all stomach, with very short legs. From morning till night she sang songs which were alternately indecent or sentimental in a harsh voice, told silly, interminable tales and only stopped talking in order to eat, or left off eating in order to talk. She was never still, was as active as a squirrel, in spite of her fat and her short legs, and her laugh, which was a torrent of shrill cries, resounded here and there, ceaselessly, in a bedroom, in the loft, in the café, everywhere, and always about nothing.

The two women on the ground floor were Louise, who was nicknamed "la Cocotte,"[1] and Flora, whom they called "Balançière,"[2] because she limped a little. The former always dressed as Liberty with a tricolored sash, and the other as a Spanish woman with a string of copper coins, which jingled at every step she took, in her carroty hair. Both looked like cooks dressed up for the carnival and were like all other women of the lower orders, neither uglier nor better looking than they usually are. In fact, they looked just like servants at an inn and were generally called the "Two Pumps."

A jealous peace, very rarely disturbed, reigned among these five women, thanks to Madame's conciliatory wisdom and to her constant good humor; and the establishment, which was the only one of the kind in the little town, was very much frequented. Madame had succeeded in giving it such a respectable appearance; she was so amiable and obliging to everybody; her good heart was so well known, that she was treated with a certain amount of consideration. The regular customers spent money on her and were delighted when she was especially friendly toward them. When they met during the day they would say: "This evening, you know where," just as men say: "At the café after dinner." In a word, Madame Tellier's house was somewhere to go to, and her customers very rarely missed their daily meetings there.

One evening toward the end of May the first arrival, M. Poulin, who was a timber merchant and had been mayor, found the door shut. The litle lantern behind the grating was not alight; there was not a sound in the house; everything seemed dead. He knocked gently at first, and then more loudly, but nobody answered the door. Then he

---

[1] Slang for a lady of easy virtue.
[2] Swing, org seesaw.

went slowly up the street, and when he got to the market place he met M. Duvert, the gunmaker, who was going to the same place, so they went back together but did not meet with any better success. But suddenly they heard a loud noise close to them, and on going round the corner of the house they saw a number of English and French sailors who were hammering at the closed shutters of the café with their fists.

The two tradesmen immediately made their escape, for fear of being compromised, but a low *pst* stopped them; it was M. Tournevau, the fish curer, who had recognized them and was trying to attract their attention. They told him what had happened, and he was all the more vexed at it, as he, a married man and father of a family, only went there on Saturdays—*securitatis causa*, as he said, alluding to a measure of sanitary policy which his friend Dr Borde had advised him to observe. That was his regular evening, and now he would be deprived of it for the whole week.

The three men went as far as the quary together, and on the way they met young M. Philippe, the banker's son, who frequented the place regularly, and M. Pinipesse, the collector. They all returned to the Rue aux Juifs together to make a last attempt. But the exasperated sailors were besieging the house, throwing stones at the shutters and shouting, and the five first-floor customers went away as quickly as possible and walked aimlessly about the streets.

Presently they met M. Dupuis, the insurance agent, and then M. Vassi, the judge of the tribunal of commerce, and they all took a long walk, going to the pier first of all. There they sat down in a row on the granite parapet and watched the rising tide, and when the promenaders had sat there for some time, M. Tournevau said: "This is not very amusing!"

"Decidedly not," M. Pinipesse replied, and they started off to walk again.

After going through the street on the top of the hill, they returned over the wooden bridge which crosses the Retenue, passed close to the railway and came out again onto the market place, when suddenly a quarrel arose between M. Pinipesse and M. Tournevau about an edible fungus which one of them declared he had found in the neighborhood.

As they were out of temper already from annoyance, they would very probably have come to blows if the others had not interfered. M. Pinipesse went off furious, and soon another altercation arose between the ex-mayor, M. Poulin and M. Dupuis, the insurance agent, on the subject of the tax collector's salary and the profits which he might make. Insulting remarks were freely passing between them when a torrent of formidable cries were heard, and the body of sailors, who were tired of waiting so long outside a closed house, came into the square. They were walking arm in arm, two and two, and formed a long procession and were shouting furiously. The landsmen went and hid themselves under a gateway, and the yelling crew disappeared in the direction of the abbey. For a long time they still heard the noise which diminished like a storm in the distance, and then silence was restored. M. Poulin and M. Dupuis, who were enraged with each other, went in different directions without wishing each other good-by.

The other four set off again and instinctively went in the direction of Mme Tellier's establishment which was still closed, silent, impenetrable. A quiet, but obstinate drunken man was knocking at the door of the café; then he stopped and called Frederic, the waiter, in a low voice, but finding that he got no answer, he sat down on the doorstep and awaited the course of events.

The others were just going to retire when the noisy band of sailors reappeared at the end of the street. The French sailors were shouting the "Marseillaise," and the Englishmen, "Rule Britannia." There was a general lurching against the wall, and then the drunken brutes went on their way toward the quay, where a fight broke out between the two nations in the course of which an Englishman had his arm broken and a Frenchman his nose split.

The drunken man who had stopped outside the door was crying by this time, as drunken men and children cry when they are vexed, and the others went away. By degrees calm was restored in the noisy town; here and there at moments the distant sound of voices could be heard, only to die away in the distance.

One man was still wandering about, M. Tournevau, the fish curer, who was vexed at having to wait until the next Saturday. He hoped for something to turn up; he did not know what, but he was exasperated at the police for thus allowing an establishment of such public utility, which they had under their control, to be thus closed.

He went back to it, examined the walls and tried to find out the reason. On the shutter he saw a notice stuck up, so he struck a wax vesta and read the following in a large, uneven hand: "Closed on account of the confirmation."

Then he went away, as he saw it was useless to remain, and left the drunken man lying on the pavement, fast asleep, outside the inhospitable door.

The next day all the regular customers, one after the other, found some reason for going through the Rue aux

Juifs with a bundle of papers under their arm, to keep them in countenance, and with a furtive glance they all read that mysterious notice:

> CLOSED ON ACCOUNT OF THE
> CONFIRMATION

II

Madame had a brother who was a carpenter in their native place, Virville, in the department of Eure. When Madame had still kept the inn at Yvetot she had stood godmother to that brother's daughter, who had received the name of Constance, Constance Rivet, she herself being a Rivet on her father's side. The carpenter, who knew that his sister was in a good position, did not lose sight of her, although they did not meet often, as they were both kept at home by their occupations and lived a long way from each other. But when the girl was twelve years old and about to be confirmed, he seized the opportunity to write to his sister and ask her to come and be present at the ceremony. Their old parents were dead, and as Madame could not well refuse, she accepted the invitation. Her brother, whose name was Joseph, hoped that by dint of showing his sister attentions she might be induced to make her will in the girl's favor, as she had no children of her own.

His sister's occupation did not trouble his scruples in the least, and, besides, nobody knew anything about it at Virville. When they spoke of her they only said: "Madame Tellier is living at Fécamp," which might mean that she was living on her own private income. It was quite twenty leagues from Fécamp to Virville, and for a peasant twenty leagues on land are more than is crossing the ocean to an educated person. The people at Virville had never been farther than Rouen, and nothing attracted the people from Fécamp to a village of five hundred houses in the middle of a plain and situated in another department. At any rate, nothing was know about her business.

But the confirmation was coming on, and Madame was in great embarrassment. She had no undermistress and did not all dare to leave her house, even for a day. She feared the rivalries between the girls upstairs and those downstairs would certainly break out; that Frederic would get drunk, for when he was in that state he would knock anybody down for a mere word. At last, however, she made up her mind to take them all with her with the exception of the man, to whom she gave a holiday until the next day but one.

When she asked her brother he made no objection but undertook to put them all up for a night. So on Saturday morning the eight o'clock express carried off Madame and her companions in a second-class carriage. As far as Beuzeille they were alone and chattered like magpies, but at that station a couple got in. The man, an aged peasant dressed in a blue blouse with a folding collar, wide sleeves, tight at the wrist and ornamented with white embroidery, wore an old high hat with long nap. He held an enormous green umbrella in one hand and a large basket in the other, from which the heads of three frightened ducks protruded. The woman, who sat stiffly in her rustic finery, had a face like a fowl and a nose that was as pointed as a bill. She sat down opposite her husband and did not stir as she was startled at finding herself in such smart company.

There was certainly an array of striking colors in the

carriage. Madame was dressed in blue silk from head to foot and had over her dress a dazzling red shawl of imitation French cashmere, Fernande was panting in a Scottish-plaid dress whose bodice, which her companions had laced as tight as they could, had forced up her falling bosom into a double dome that was continually heaving up and down and which seemed liquid beneath the material. Raphaelle, with a bonnet covered with feathers so that it looked like a nestful of birds, had on a lilac dress with gold spots on it; there was something oriental about it that suited her Jewish face. Rosa the Jade had on a pink petticoat with large flounces and looked like a very fat child, an obese dwarf, while the Two Pumps looked as if they had cut their dresses out of old flowered curtains, dating from the Restoration.

Perceiving that they were no longer alone in the compartment, the ladies put on staid looks and began to talk of subjects which might give the others a high opinion of them. But at Bolbec a gentleman with light whiskers, with a gold chain and wearing two or three rings, got in and put several parcels wrapped in oilcloth into the net over his head. He looked inclined for a joke and a good-natured fellow.

"Are you ladies changing your quarters?" he asked. The question embarrassed them all considerably. Madame, however, quickly recovered her composure and said sharply, to avenge the honor of her corps:

"I think you might try and be polite!"

He excused himself and said: "I beg your pardon; I ought to have said your nunnery."

As Madame could not think of a retort, or perhaps as she thought herself justified sufficiently, she gave him a dignified bow and pinched in her lips.

Then the gentleman, who was sitting between Rosa the Jade and the old peasant, began to wink knowingly at the ducks, whose heads were sticking out of the basket. When he felt that he had fixed the attention of his public he began to tickle them under their bills and spoke funnily to them, to make the company smile.

"We have left our little pond, qu-ack! qu-ack! to make the acquaintance of the little spit, qu-ack! qu-ack!"

The unfortunate creatures turned their necks away to avoid his caresses and made desperate efforts to get out of their wicker prison and then suddenly, all at once, uttered the most lamentable quacks of distress. The women exploded with laughter. They leaned forward and pushed each other so as to see better; they were very much interested in the ducks, and the gentleman redoubled his airs, his witt and his teasing.

Rosa joined in and, leaning over her neighbor's legs, she kissed the three animals on the head. Immediately all the girls wanted to kiss them in turn, and the gentleman took them onto his knees, made them jump up and down and pinched them. The two peasants, who were even in greater consternation than their poultry, rolled their eyes as if they were possessed, without venturing to move, and their old wrinkled faces had not a smile or a movement.

Then the gentleman, who was a commercial traveler, offered the ladies braces by way of a joke and, taking up one of his packages, he opened it. It was a trick, for the parcel contained garters. There were blue silk, pink silk, red silk, violet silk, mauve silk garters, and the buckles were made of two gilt metal Cupids embracing each other. The girls uttered exclamations of delight and looked at them with that gravity which is natural to a woman when she is hankering after a bargain. They consulted one another by their looks or in a whisper and replied in the same manner, and madame was longingly handling a pair of orange garters that were broader and more imposing than the rest, really fit for the mistress of such an establishment.

"Come, my kittens," he said, "you must try them on."

There was a torrent of exclamations, and they squeezed their petticoats between their legs, as if they thought he was going to ravish them, but he quiety waited his time and said: "Well, if you will not I shall pack them up again."

And he added cunningly: "I offer my pair they like to those who will try them on."

But they would not and sat up very straight and looked dignified.

But the Two Pumps looked so distressed that he renewed the offer to them. Flora especially hesitated, and he pressed her:

"Come, my dear, a little courage! Just look at that lilac pair; it will suit your dress admirably."

That decided her and, pulling up her dress, she showed a thick leg, fit for a milkmaid, in a badly fitting coarse stocking. The commercial traveler stooped down and fastened the garter below the knee first of all and then above it, and he tickled the girl gently, which made her scream and jump. When he had done he gave her the lilac pair and asked: "Who next?"

"I! I!" they all shouted at once, and he began on Rosa the Jade, who uncovered a shapeless, round thing without any ankle, a regular "sausage of a leg," as Raphaelle used to say.

The commercial traveler complimented Fernande and grew quite enthusiastic over her powerful columns.

The thin tibias of the handsome Jewess met with less

flattery, and Louise Cocotte, by way of a joke, put her petticoats over the man's head, so that Madame was obliged to interfere to check such unseemly behavior.

Lastly Madame herself put out her leg, a handsome, muscular Norman leg, and in his surprise and pleasure the commercial traveler gallantly took off his hat to salute that master calf, like a true French cavalier.

The two peasants, who were speechless from surprise, looked askance out of the corners of their eyes. They looked so exactly like fowls that the man with the light whiskers, when he sat up, said, "Co–co–ri–co" under their very noses, and that gave rise to another storm of amusement.

The old people got out at Motteville with their basket, their ducks and their umbrella, and they heard the woman say to her husband as they went away:

"They are sluts who are off to that cursed place, Paris."

The funny commercial traveler himself got out at Rouen, after behaving so coarsely that Madame was obliged sharply to put him into his right place. She added as a moral: "This will teach us not to talk to the firstcomer."

At Oissel they changed trains, and at a little station farther on M. Joseph Rivet was waiting for them with a large cart and a number of chairs in it, which was drawn by a white horse.

The carpenter politely kissed all the ladies and then helped them into his conveyance.

Three of them sat on three cairs at the back, Raphaelle, Madame and her brother on the three chairs in front, and Rosa, who had no seat, settled herself as comfortably as she could on tall Fernande's knees, and then they set off.

But the horse's jerky trot shook the cart so terribly that the chairs began to dance, throwing the travelers into the air, to the right and to the left, as if they had been dancing puppets. This made them make horrible grimaces and screams, which, however, were cut short by another jolt of the cart.

They clung to the sides of the vehicle; their bonnets fell onto their backs, their noses on their shoulders, and the white horse trotted on, stretching out his head and holding out his tail quite straight, a little hairless rat's tail, with which he whisked his buttocks from time to time.

Joseph Rivet, with one leg on the shafts and the other bent under him, held the reins with elbows high and kept uttering a kind of chuckling sound which made the horse prick up its ears and go faster.

The green country extended on either side of the road, and here and there the colza in flower presented a waving expanse of yellow, from which there arose a strong, wholesome, sweet and penetrating smell which the wind carried to some distance.

The cornflowers showed their little blue heads among the rye, and the women wanted to pick them, but M. Rivet refused to stop.

Then sometimes a whole field appeared to be covered with blood, so thickly were the poppies growing, and the cart, which looked as if it were filled with flowers of more brilliant hue, drove on through the fields colored with wild flowers, to disappear behind the trees of a farm, then to reappear and go on again through the yellow or green standing crops studded with red or blue.

One o'clock struck as they drove up to the carpenter's door. They were tired out and very hungry, as they had eatern nothing since they left home. Madame Rivet ran out and made them alight, one after another, kissing them as soon as they were on the grounds. She seemed as if she would never tire of kissing her sister-in-law, whom she apparently wanted to monopolize. They had lunch in the workshop, which had been cleared out for the next day's dinner.

A capital omelet, followed by boiled chitterlings and washed down by good sharp cider, made them all feel comfortable.

Rivet had taken a glass so that he might hobnob with them, and his wife cooked, waited on them, brought in the dishes, took them out and asked all of them in a whisper whether they had everything they wanted. A number of boards standing against the walls and heaps of shavings that had been swept into the corners gave out the smell of planed wood, of carpentering, that resinous odor which penetrates the lungs.

They wanted to see the little girl, but she had gone to church and would not be back until evening, so they all went out for a stroll in the country.

It was a small village through which the high road passed. Ten of a dozen houses on either side of the single street had for tenants the butcher, the grocer, the carpenter, the innkeeper, the shoemaker and the baker and others.

The church was at the end of the street. It was surrounded by a small churchyard, and four enormous lime trees which stood just outside the porch shaded it completely. It was built of flint, in no particular style, and had a slated steeple. When you got past it you were in the open country again, which was broken here and there by clumps of trees which hid some home-stead.

Rivet had given his arm to his sister out of politeness, although he was in his working clothes, and was walking with her majestically. His wife, who was overwhelmed by Raphaelle's gold-striped dress, was walking between her and Fernande, and rotund Rosa was trotting behind with Louise Cocotte and Flora, the seesaw, who was limping along, quite tired out.

The inhabitants came to their dors; the children left off playing, and a window curtain would be raised so as to show a muslin cap, while an old woman with a crutch, who was almost blind, crossed herself as if it were a religious procession. They all looked for a long time after those handsome ladies from the town who had come so far to be present at the confirmation of Joseph Rivet's little girl, and the carpenter rose very much in the public estimation.

As they passed the church they heard some children singing; little shrill voices were singing a hymn, but Madame would not let them go in for fear of disturbing the little cherubs.

After a walk, during which Joseph Rivet enumerated the principal landed proprietors, spoke about the yield of the land and the productiveness of the cows and sheep, he took his flock of women home and installed them in his house, and as it was very small, he had put them into the rooms two and two.

Just for once Rivet would sleep in the workshop on the shavings; his wife was going to share her bed with her sister-in-law, and Fernande and Raphaelle were to sleep together in the next room. Louise and Flora were put into the kitchen, where they had a mattress on the floor, and Rosa had a little dark cupboard at the top of the stairs to herself, close to the loft, where the candidate for confirmation was to sleep.

When the girl came in she was overwhelmed with

kisses; all the women wished to caress her with that need of tender expansion, that habit of professional wheedling which had made them kiss the ducks in the railway carriage.

They took her onto their laps, stroked her soft, light hair and pressed her in their arms with vehement and spontaneous outbursts of affection, and the child, who was very good natured and docile, bore it all patiently.

As the day had been a fatiguing one for everybody, they all went to bed soon after dinner. The whole village was wrapped in that perfect stillness of the country, which is almost like a religious silence, and the girls, who were accustomed to the noisy evenings of their establishment, felt rather impressed by the perfect repose of the sleeping village. They shivered, not with cold, but with those little shivers of solitude which come over uneasy and troubled hearts.

As soon as they were in bed, two and two together, they clasped each other in their arms, as if to protect themselves against this feeling of the calm and profound slumber of the earth. But Rosa the Jade, who was alone. in her little dark cupboard, felt a vague and painful emotion come over her.

She was tossing about in bed, unable to get to sleep, when she heard the faint sobs of a crying child close to her head through the partition. She was frightened and called out and was answered by a weak voice, broken by sobs. It was the little girl who, being used to sleeping in her mother's room, was frightened in her small attic.

Rosa was delighted, got up softly so as not to awaken anyone and went and fetched the child. She took her into her warm bed, kissed her and pressed her to her bosom, caressed her, lavished exaggerated manifestations of tenderness on her and at last grew calmer herself and went to sleep. And till morning the candidate for confirmation slept with her head on Rosa's naked bosom.

At five o'clock the little church bell ringing the Angelus woke these women up, who as a rule slept the whole morning long.

The peasants were up already, and the women went busily from house to house, carefully bringing short, starched muslin dresses in bandboxes, or very long wax tapers with a bow of silk fringed with gold in the middle and with dents in the wax for the fingers.

The sun was already high in the blue sky which still had a rosy tint toward the horizon, like a faint trace of dawn, remaining. Families of fowls were walking about the hen houses, and here and there a black cock with a glistening breast raised his head, crowned by his red comb, flapped his wings and uttered his shrill crow, which the other cocks repeated.

Vehicles of all sorts came from neighboring parishes and discharged tall Norman women in dark dresses, with neck handkerchiefs crossed over the bosom and fastened with silver brooches, a hundred years old.

The men had put on blouses over their new frock coats or over their old dress coats of green cloth, the tails of which hung down below their blouses. When the horses were in the stable there was a double line of rustic conveyances along the road: carts, cabriolets, tilburies, charabancs, traps of every shape and age, resting on their shafts or pointing them in the air.

The carpenter's house was as busy as a beehive. The ladies, in dressing jackets and petticoats, with their long, thin, light hair which looked as if it were faded and worn by dyeing, were busy dressing the child, who was standing motionless on a table while Madame Tellier was directing the movements of her battalion. They washed her, did her hair, dressed her, and with the help of a number of pins they arranged the folds of her dress and took in the waist, which was too large.

Then when she was ready she was told to sit down and not to move, and the women hurried off to get ready themselves.

The church bell began to ring again, and its tinkle was lost in the air, like a feeble voice which is soon drowned in space. The candidates came out of the houses and went toward the parochial building which contained the school and the mansion house. This stood quite at one end of the village, while the church was situated at the other.

The parents, in their very best clothes, followed their children with awkward looks and with the clumsy movements of bodies that are always bent at work.

The little girls disappeared in a cloud of muslin which looked like whipped cream, while the lads, who looked like embryo waiters in a café and whose heads shone with pomatum, walked with their legs apart, so as not to get any dust or dirt onto their black trousers.

It was something for the family to be proud of; a large number of relatives from distant parts surrounded the child, and consequently the carpenter's triumph was complete.

Mme Tellier's regiment, with its mistress as its head, followed Constance; her father gave his arm to his sister; her mother walked by the side of Raphaelle, Fernande with Rosa, and the Two Pumps together. Thus they walked majestically through the village, like a general's staff in full uniform, while the effect on the village was startling.

At the school the girls arranged themselves under the

Sister of Mercy and the boys under the schoolmaster, and they started off, singing a hymn as they went. The boys led the way in two files between the two rows of vehicles, from which the horses had been taken out, and the girls followed in the same order. As all the people in the village had given the town ladies the precedence out of politeness, they came immediately behind the girls and lengthened the double line of the procession still more, three on the right and three on the left, while their dresses were as striking as a bouquet of fireworks.

When they went into the church the congregation grew quite excited. They pressed against each other; they turned round; they jostled one another in order to see. Some of the devout ones almost spoke aloud, so astonished were they at the sight of these ladies, whose dresses were trimmed more elaborately than the priest's chasuble.

The mayor offered them his pew, the first one on the right, close to the choir, and Mme Tellier sat there with her sister-in-law; Fernande and Raphaelle, Rosa the Jade and the Two Pumps occupied the second seat, in company with the carpenter.

The choir was full of kneeling children, the girls on one side and the boys on the other, and the long wax tapers which they held looked like lances, pointing in all directions. Three men were standing in front of the lectern, singing as loud as they could.

They prolonged the syllables of the sonorous Latin indefinitely, holding on to the amens with interminable *a–as*, which the serpent of the organ kept up in the monotonous, long-drawn-out notes, emitted by the deep-throated pipes.

A child's shrill voice took up the reply, and from time to time a priest sitting in a stall and wearing a biretta got up, muttered something and sat down again. The three singers continued, with their eyes fixed on the big book of plain song lying open before them on the outstretched wings of an eagle mounted on a pivot.

Then silence ensued. The service went on, and toward the end of it Rosa, with her head in both her hands, suddenly thought of her mother and her village church on a similar occasion. She almost fancied that that day had returned when she was so small and almost hidden in her white dress, and she began to cry.

First of all she wept silently; the tears dropped slowly from her eyes, but her emotion increased with her recollections, and she began to sob. She took out her pocket handkerchief, wiped her eyes and held it to her mouth so as not to scream, but it was useless.

A sort of rattle escaped her throat, and she was answered by two other profound, heartbreaking sobs; for her two neighbors, Louise and Flora, who were kneeling near her, overcome by similar recollections, were sobbing by her side. There was a flood of tears, and as weeping is contagious, Madame soon found that her eyes were wet and on turning to her sister-in-law she saw that all the occupants of the pew were crying.

Soon throughout the church here and there a wife, a mother, a sister, seized by the strange sympathy of poignant emotion and agitated by the grief of those handsome ladies on their knees who were shaken by their sobs, was moistening her cambric pocket handkerchief and pressing her beating heart with her left hand.

Just as the sparks from an engine will set fire to dry grass, so the tears of Rosa and of her companions infected the whole congregation in a moment. Men, women, old men and lads in new blouses were soon sobbing;

something superhuman seemed to be hovering over their heads—a spirit, the powerful breath of an invisible and all-powerful being.

Suddenly a species of madness seemed to pervade the church, the noise of a crowd in a state of frenzy, a tempest of sobs and of stifled cries. It passed over the people like gusts of wind which bow the trees in a forest, and the priest, overcome by emotion, stammered out incoherent prayers, those inarticulate prayers of the soul when it soars toward heaven.

The people behind him gradually grew calmer. The cantors, in all the dignity of their white surplices, went on in somewhat uncertain voices, and the organ itself seemed hoarse, as if the instrument had been weeping. The priest, however, raised his hand as a sign for them to be still and went to the chancel steps. All were silent immediately.

After a few remarks on what had just taken place, which he attributed to a miracle, he continued, turning to the seats where the carpenter's guests were sitting:

"I especially thank you, my dear sisters, who have come from such a distance and whose presence among us, whose evident faith and ardent piety have set such a salutary example to all. You have edified my parish; your emotion has warmed all hearts; without you this day would not, perhaps, have had this really divine character. It is sufficient at times that there should be one chosen to keep in the flock, to make the whole flock blessed."

His voice failed him again from emotion, and he said no more but concluded the service.

They all left the church as quickly as possible; the children themselves were restless, tired with such a prolonged tension of the mind. Besides, the elders were hungry, and one after another left the churchyard to see about dinner.

There was a crowd outside, a noisy crowd, a babel of loud voices in which the shrill Norman accent was discernible. The villagers formed two ranks, and when the children appeared each family seized their own.

The whole houseful of women caught hold of Constance, surrounded her and kissed her, and Rosa was especially demonstrative. At last she took hold of one hand, while Mme Tellier held the other, and Raphaelle and Fernande held up her long muslin petticoat so that it might not drag in the dust. Louise and Flora brought up the rear with Mme Rivet, and the child, who was very silent and thoughtful, set off home in the midst of this guard of honor.

The dinner was served in the workshop on long boards supported by trestles, and through the open door they could see all the enjoyment that was going on. Everywhere people were feasting; through every window could be seen tables surrounded by people in their Sunday clothes. There was merriment in every house—men sitting in their shirt sleeves, drinking cider, glass after glass.

In the carpenter's house the gaiety took on somewhat of an air of reserve, the consequence of the emotion of the girls in the morning. Rivet was the only one who was in good cue, and he was drinking to excess. Mme Tellier was looking at the clock every moment, for in order not to lose two days following they ought to take the 3:55 train, which would bring them to Fécamp by dark.

The carpenter tried very hard to distract her attention so as to keep his guests until the next day. But he did not succeed, for she never joked when there was business to be done, and as soon as they had had their coffee she ordered her girls to make haste and get ready. Then, turning to her brother, she said:

"You must have the horse put in immediately," and she herself went to complete her preparations.

When she came down again her sister-in-law was waiting to speak to her about the child, and a long conversation took place in which, however, nothing was settled. The carpenter's wife finessed and pretended to be very much moved, and Mme Tellier, who was holding the girl on her knees, would not pledge herself to anything definite but merely gave vague promises: she would not forget her; there was plenty of time, and then, they were sure to meet again.

But the conveyance did not come to the door, and the women did not come downstairs. Upstairs they even heard loud laughter, falls, little screams and much clapping of hands, and so while the carpenter's wife went to the stable to see whether the cart was ready Madame went upstairs.

Rivet, who was very drunk and half undressed, was vainly trying to kiss Rosa, who was choking with laughter. The Two Pumps were holding him by the arms and trying to calm him, as they were shocked at such a scene after that morning's ceremony, but Raphaelle and Fernande were urging him on, writhing and holding their sides with laughter, and they uttered shrill cries at every useless attempt that the drunken fellow made.

The man was furious; his face was red; his dress disordered, and he was trying to shake off the two women who were clinging to him while he was pulling Rosa's bodice with all his might and ejaculating: "Won't you, you slut?"

But Madame, who was very indignant, went up to her brother, seized him by the shoulders and threw him out of the room with such violence that he fell against a wall in the passage, and a minute afterward they heard him pumping water onto his head in the yard. When he came back with the cart he was already quite calmed down.

They seated themselves in the country; the roads were glaring and dazzled their eyes. The wheels raised up two trails of dust which followed the cart for a long time along the highroad, and presently Fernande, who was fond of music, asked Rosa to sing something. She boldly struck up the "*Gros Curé de Meudon*," but Madame made her stop immediately, as she thought it a song which was very unsuitable for such a day, and added:

"Sing us something of Béranger's."

After a moment's hesitation Rosa began Béranger's song, "The Grandmother," in her worn-out voice, and all the girls, and even Madame herself, joined in the chorus:

> "*How I regret*
> *My dimpled arms,*
> *My well-made legs,*
> *And my vanished charms!*"

"That is first-rate," Rivet declared, carried away by the rhythm. They shouted the refrain to every verse, while Rivet beat time on the shafts with his foot and on the horse's back with the reins. The animal himself, carried away by the rhythm, broke into a wild gallop and threw all the women in a heap, one on top of the other, in the bottom of the conveyance.

They got up, laughing as if they were crazy, and the song went on, shouted at the top of their voices, beneath the burning sky and among the ripening grain, to the rapid gallop of the little horse who set off every time the refrain was sung and galloped a hundred yards, to their great delight. Occasionally a stone breaker by the roadside sat up and looked at the wild and shouting female load through his wire spectacles.

When they got out at the station the carpenter said:

"I am sorry you are going; we might have had some fun together."

But Madame replied very sensibly: "Everything has its right time, and we cannot always be enjoying ourselves."

And then he had a sudden inspiration: "Look here, I will come and see you at Fécamp next month." And he gave a knowing look with his bright and rougish eyes.

"Come," Madame said, "you must be sensible; you may come if you like, but you are not to be up to any of your tricks."

He did not reply, and as they heard the whistle of the train he immediately began to kiss them all. When it came to Rosa's turn he tried to get to her mouth which she, however, smiling with her lips closed, turned away from him each time by a rapid movement of her head to one side. He held her in his arms, but he could not attain his object as his large whip, which he was holding in his hand and waving behind the girl's back in desperation, interfered with his efforts.

"Passengers for Rouen, take your seats, please!" a guard cried, and they got in. There was a slight whistle, followed by a loud one from the engine, which noisily puffed out its first jet of steam while the wheels began to turn a little with visible effort. Rivet left the station and went to the gate by the side of the line to get another look at Rosa, and as the carriage full of human merchandise passed him he began to crack his whip and to jump, singing at the top of his voice:

> *"How I regret*
> *My dimpled arms,*
> *My well-made legs,*
> *And my vanished charms!"*

And then he watched a white pocket handkerchief which somebody was waving as it disappeared in the distance.

III

They slept the peaceful sleep of quiet consciences until they got to Rouen. When they returned to the house, refreshed, and rested, Madame could not help saying:

"It was all very well, but I was already longing to get home."

They hurried over their supper, and then, when they had put on their usual light evening costumes, waited for their usual customers. The little colored lamp outside the door told the passers-by that the flock had returned to the fold, and in a moment the news spread; nobody knew how or by whom.

M. Philippe, the banker's son, even carried his audacity so far as to send a special messenger to M. Tournevau, who was in the bosom of his family.

The fish curer used every Sunday to have several cousins to dinner, and they were having coffee, when a man came in with a letter in his hand. M. Tournevau was much excited; he opened the envelope and grew pale; it only contained these words in pencil:

The cargo of fish has been found; the ship has come into port; good business for you. Come immediately.

He felt in his pockets, gave the messenger twopence and, suddenly blushing to his ears, he said: "I must go out." He handed his wife the laconic and mysterious note, rang the bell, and when the servant came in he asked her to bring him his hat and overcoat immediately. As soon as he was in the street he began to run, and the way seemed to him to be twice as long as usual, in consequence of his impatience.

Mme Tellier's establishment had put on quite a holiday look. On the ground floor a number of sailors were making a deafening noise, and Louise and Flora drank with one and the other so as to merit their name of the Two Pumps more than ever. They were being called for everywhere at once; already they were not quite sober enough for their business, and the night bid fair to be a very jolly one.

The upstairs room was full by nine o'clock. M. Vassi, the judge of the tribunal of commerce, Madame's usual platonic wooer, was talking to her in a corner in a low voice, and they were both smiling, as if they were about to come to an understanding.

M. Poulin, the ex-mayor, was holding Rosa on his knees, and she, with her nose close to his, was running her hands through the old gentleman's white whiskers.

Tall Fernande, who was lying on the sofa, had both her feet on M. Pinipesse the tax collector's stomach and her back on young M. Philippe's waistcoat; her right arm was round his neck, and she held a cigarette in her left.

Raphaelle appeared to be discussing matters with M. Dupuis, the insurance agent, and she finished by saying: "Yes, my dear, I will."

Just then the door opened suddenly, and M. Tournevau came in. He was greeted with enthusiastic cries of: "Long live Tournevau!" And Raphaelle, who was twirling around, went and threw herself into his arms. He seized her in a vigorous embrace, and without saying a word, lifting her up as if she had been a feather, he carried her through the room.

Rosa was chatting to the ex-mayor, kissing him every moment and pulling both his whiskers at the same time in order to keep his head straight.

Fernande and Madame remained with the four men, and M. Philippe exclaimed: "I will pay for some champagne; get three bottles, Madame Tellier." And Fernande gave him a hug and whispered to him: "Play us a waltz, will you?" So he rose and sat down at the old piano in the corner and managed to get a hoarse waltz out of the entrails of the instrument.

The tall girl put her arms round the tax collector, Madame asked M. Vassi to take her in his arms, and the two couples turned round, kissing as they danced. M. Vassi, who had formerly danced in good society, waltzed with such elegance that Madame was quite captivated.

Frederic brought the champagne; the first cork popped, and M. Philippe played the introduction to a quadrille, through which the four dancers walked in society fashion, decorously, with propriety of deportment, with bows and curtsies, and then they began to drink.

M. Philippe next struck up a lively polka, and M. Tournevau started off with the handsome Jewess whom he held up in the air without letting her feet touch the ground. M. Pinipesse and M. Vassi had started off with renewed vigor, and from time to time one or other couple would stop to toss off a long glass of sparkling wine. The dance was threatening to become never ending, when Rosa opened the door.

"I want to dance," she exclaimed. And she caught hold

of M. Dupuis, who was sitting idle on the couch, and the dance began again.

But the bottles were empty. "I will pay for one," M. Tournevau said.

"So will I," M. Vassi declared.

"And I will do the same," M. Dupuis remarked.

Then all began to clap their hands, and it soon became a regular ball. From time to time Louise and Flora ran upstairs quickly, had a few turns while their customers downstairs grew impatient, and then they returned regretfully to the café. At midnight they were still dancing.

Madame shut her eyes to what was going on, and she had long private talks in corners with M. Vassi, as if to settle the last details of something that had already been agreed upon.

At last at one o'clock the two married men, M. Tournevau and M. Pinipesse, declared that they were going home and wanted to pay. Nothing was charged for except the champagne, and that only cost six francs a bottle instead of ten, which was the usual price, and when they expressed their surprise at such generosity Madame, who was beaming, said to them:

"We don't have a holiday every day."